A Way Out of No Way

Here are some other Edge Books
from Henry Holt you will enjoy:

AMERICAN EYES
New Asian-American Short Stories
for Young Adults
edited by Lori M. Carlson

BARRIO STREETS CARNIVAL DREAMS
Three Generations of Latino Artistry
edited by Lori M. Carlson

COOL SALSA
Bilingual Poems on Growing Up Latino
in the United States
edited by Lori M. Carlson

DAMNED STRONG LOVE
The True Story of Willi G. and Stefan K.
by Lutz van Dijk
translated from the German by Elizabeth D. Crawford

THE LONG SEASON OF RAIN
by Helen Kim

ONE BIRD
by Kyoko Mori

A Way Out of No Way

WRITINGS ABOUT GROWING UP BLACK IN AMERICA

EDITED BY

Jacqueline Woodson

HENRY HOLT AND COMPANY • NEW YORK

Henry Holt and Company, Inc.
Publishers since 1866
115 West 18th Street
New York, New York 10011

Henry Holt is a registered
trademark of Henry Holt and Company, Inc.

Published in Canada by Fitzhenry & Whiteside Ltd.,
195 Allstate Parkway, Markham, Ontario L3R 4T8.

Library of Congress Cataloging-in-Publication Data
A way out of no way: writings about growing up black in
America / edited by Jacqueline Woodson.
p. cm.—(Edge Books)
Summary: A collection of stories and poems about
coming of age written by Afro-American authors.
1. Afro-Americans—Literary collections. 2. Children's literature,
American—Afro-American authors. [1. Afro-Americans—
Literary collections. 2. American literature—Afro-American
authors—Collections.] I. Woodson, Jacqueline. II. Series.
PZ5.W295 1996
[Fic]—dc20 96-7891

ISBN 0-8050-4570-8
Designed by Victoria Hartman
First Edition—1996

Printed in the United States of America
on acid-free paper. ∞
10 9 8 7 6 5 4 3 2 1

OVER THE WATER
by Maude Casey

THE REBELLIOUS ALPHABET
by Jorge Diaz
translated from the Spanish by Geoffrey Fox

THE ROLLER BIRDS OF RAMPUR
by Indi Rana

SHIZUKO'S DAUGHTER
by Kyoko Mori

THE SONG OF BE
by Lesley Beake

SPYGLASS
An Autobiography
by Hélène Deschamps

WE ARE WITNESSES
The Diaries of Five Teenagers Who Died in the Holocaust
by Jacob Boas

For the writers

who came before me

and the writers who

are on their way

Thanks so much to

Catherine McKinley, Marc Aronson,

Matt Rosen, Kathryn Haber, Toshi Reagon,

Charlotte Sheedy, and, of course, my family—

especially, Linda Villarosa and Jill Harris

Contents

But I sighted a distant horizon. . . .

I battered the cordons around me. . . .

A Way Out of No Way

Introduction

IMAGINE BROOKLYN on a warm autumn afternoon. Double Dutch ropes clicking. Freeze tag players running from base to base—from lamppost to hydrant to the blue parked car on the corner. And from a high-up window, the sound of music—so full of bass the words are indiscernible, but it doesn't matter because down below, spilling out onto the curb, a dozen teenagers are dancing. Imagine my Brooklyn—the place of my childhood.

Imagine the 1970s. The Vietnam War. The Black Panthers. The Funkadelics. Sly and the Family Stone. Afros and platform shoes. Gumby and click clacks. "Soul Train" and Cadillacs.

Imagine a room the size of a large closet. One window beside a door leading to a backyard. A single bed. A narrow dresser. Another door leading to an expansive kitchen. And in the kitchen, siblings gathered around a table large enough to hold the weight and chaos of this family. Imagine books and notebooks and forged letters from parents, pens and pencils, half-empty Pepsi cans, cookie crumbs, the remains of a fried chicken leg, a fruit bowl filled with oranges and walnuts, another bowl filled with peppermints (imagine a grandmother pressing one into the sour mouth of a child), and laughter, teasing, a little bit of pain.

But we are not in that kitchen. We are in this monastic room, the door leading to the kitchen closed tight against the sound of sisters and brothers, and in the far corner of this room, me, at twelve, with the newly discovered stories of James Baldwin, Toni Cade Bambara, and Langston Hughes.

And in the room, alone with these writers, I do not know anything—that they are at this moment, as I read their words hungrily (for until this time, I had never read a story written by an African American about African Americans), introducing me to a bigger world, and making real for me my own dream of becoming a writer. And they are at this moment teaching me the worthiness of my struggles to come. So I read these works, greedily, finding the common ground in lives so much like my own but different too.

Imagine a tiny room, and in it, the spirits of black writers pointing a Brooklyn girl in the direction of her dream.

I didn't know where James Baldwin's Beale Street was, or if indeed it existed at all; but it hollered and sweated like my own street, so I read this story again and again because each time I visited Beale Street, I went home.

And Passing—I had heard the term whispered from behind down-turned adult lips, and now, here was Langston Hughes putting a story to it.

I wanted Gwendolyn Brooks's Maud Martha to move into the house next door, wanted to go to school and meet up with Ntozake Shange's Betsey Brown.

Now imagine the years have dropped away like pages. The tiny room is now a guest room in a house I have long since moved away from. Some mornings, when the world is quiet as sleep, I can listen and almost hear the echoes of my brothers' and sisters' teasing and laughter and sadness and joy.

And sometimes, a reader can listen and hear someone else's pain. Listen to "Big Bowls of Cereal." Listen to "Passing." Listen to "Ought to Be a Woman." Read and listen and realize the pain is as important as the joy. Read and listen and share another's memory.

Memory becomes the thing that connects us. In Randall Kenan's *A Visitation of Spirits*, he reminisces on a hog killing. Claude McKay tells us we must not die like hogs but must fight. And in the end, Bernice Johnson Reagon reminds us to remember it all, the good and the bad, the sweet and the sorrowful. These stories and poems take me back to the places of each writer's long, long time ago.

Yes, the years move away from us, slip into the quiet place of memory. Sitting down to write this, I realize again that remembering is about believing, believing that there is a past and therefore a future.

This morning, as I pull the books from my shelves to

re-create a sense of that tiny room that once was mine, I realize that the room has grown, and there are other voices, newer ones, and the voices continue to come—to remind me again of the past, the present, and the future. And my study fills with the spirits of these writers offering anyone who reads their words, a way out of no way: pointing a beautiful black finger toward a holy, holy place.

—Jacqueline Woodson

Your World is as big as you make it.

I know, for I used to abide

In the narrowest nest in a corner,

My wings pressing close to my side . . .

ERNEST J.
GAINES

FROM

A Lesson Before Dying

I WAS NOT THERE, yet I was there. No, I did not go to the trial, I did not hear the verdict, because I knew all the time what it would be. Still, I was there. I was there as much as anyone else was there. Either I sat behind my aunt and his godmother or I sat beside them. Both are large women, but his godmother is larger. She is of average height, five four, five five, but weighs nearly two hundred pounds. Once she and my aunt had found their places—two rows behind the table where he sat with his court-appointed attorney—his godmother became as immobile as a great stone or as one of our oak or cypress stumps. She never got up once to get water or go to the bathroom down in the basement. She just sat there staring at the boy's clean-cropped head where he sat at the front table with his lawyer. Even after he had gone to await the jurors' verdict, her eyes remained in that one direction. She heard nothing said in the courtroom. Not by the prosecutor, not by the defense attorney, not by my aunt. (Oh, yes, she did hear one word—one word, for sure: "hog.") It was my aunt whose eyes followed the prosecutor as he moved from one side of the courtroom to the other, pounding his fist into the palm of his hand, pounding the table where his papers lay, pounding the rail that separated the jurors from the rest of the courtroom. It was my aunt who followed his every move, not his godmother. She was not even listening. She had gotten tired of listening. She knew, as we all knew, what the outcome would be. A white man had been killed during a robbery, and though two of the robbers had been killed on the spot, one had been captured, and he, too, would have to die. Though he told them no, he had nothing to do with it, that he was on his way to the White Rabbit Bar and Lounge when Brother and Bear drove up beside him and offered him a ride. After he got into the car, they asked him if he had any money. When he told them he didn't have a solitary dime, it was then that Brother and Bear started talking credit, saying that old Gropé should not mind crediting them a pint since he knew them well, and he knew that the grinding season was coming soon, and they would be able to pay him back then.

The store was empty, except for the old storekeeper, Alcee Gropé, who sat on a stool behind the counter. He spoke first. He asked Jefferson about his godmother. Jefferson told him his nannan was all right. Old Gropé nodded his head. "You tell her for me I say hello," he told Jefferson. He looked at Brother and Bear. But he didn't like them. He didn't trust them. Jefferson could see that in his face. "Do for you boys?" he asked. "A bottle of that Apple White, there, Mr. Gropé," Bear said. Old Gropé got the bottle off the shelf, but he did not set it on the counter. He could see that the boys had already been drinking, and he became suspicious. "You boys got money?" he asked. Brother and Bear spread out all the money they had in their pockets on top of the counter. Old Gropé counted it with his eyes. "That's not enough," he said. "Come on, now, Mr. Gropé," they pleaded with him. "You know you go'n get your money soon as grinding start." "No," he said. "Money is slack everywhere. You bring the money, you get your wine." He turned to put the bottle back on the shelf. One of the boys, the one called Bear, started around the counter. "You, stop there," Gropé told him. "Go back." Bear had been drinking, and his eyes were glossy, he walked unsteadily, grinning all the time as he continued around the counter. "Go back," Gropé told him. "I mean, the last time now—go back." Bear continued. Gropé moved quickly toward the cash register, where he withdrew a revolver and started shooting. Soon there was shooting from another direction. When it was quiet again, Bear, Gropé, and Brother were all down on the floor, and only Jefferson was standing.

He wanted to run, but he couldn't run. He couldn't even think. He didn't know where he was. He didn't know how he had gotten there. He couldn't remember ever getting into the car. He couldn't remember a thing he had done all day.

He heard a voice calling. He thought the voice was

coming from the liquor shelves. Then he realized that old Gropé was not dead, and that it was he who was calling. He made himself go to the end of the counter. He had to look across Bear to see the storekeeper. Both lay between the counter and the shelves of alcohol. Several bottles had been broken, and alcohol and blood covered their bodies as well as the floor. He stood there gaping at the old man slumped against the bottom shelf of gallons and half gallons of wine. He didn't know whether he should go to him or whether he should run out of there. The old man continued to call: "Boy? Boy? Boy?" Jefferson became frightened. The old man was still alive. He had seen him. He would tell on him. Now he started babbling. "It wasn't me. It wasn't me, Mr. Gropé. It was Brother and Bear. Brother shot you. It wasn't me. They made me come with them. You got to tell the law that, Mr. Gropé. You hear me, Mr. Gropé?"

But he was talking to a dead man.

Still he did not run. He didn't know what to do. He didn't believe that this had happened. Again he couldn't remember how he had gotten there. He didn't know whether he had come there with Brother and Bear, or whether he had walked in and seen all this after it happened.

He looked from one dead body to the other. He didn't know whether he should call someone on the telephone or run. He had never dialed a telephone in his life, but he had seen other people use them. He didn't know what to do. He was standing by the liquor shelf, and suddenly he realized he needed a drink and needed it badly. He snatched a bottle off the shelf, wrung off the cap, and turned up the bottle, all in one continuous motion. The whiskey burned him like fire—his chest, his belly, even his nostrils. His eyes watered; he shook his head to clear his mind. Now he began to realize where he was. Now he began to realize fully what had happened. Now he knew he had to get out of there. He turned. He saw the money in the cash register, under the little wire clamps. He knew taking money was wrong. His nannan had told him never to steal. He didn't want to steal. But he didn't have a solitary dime in his pocket. And nobody was around, so who could say he stole it? Surely not one of the dead men.

He was halfway across the room, the money stuffed inside his jacket pocket, the half bottle of whiskey clutched in his hand, when two white men walked into the store.

That was his story.

The prosecutor's story was different. The prosecutor argued that Jefferson and the other two had gone there with the full intention of robbing the old man and then killing him so that he could not identify them. When the old man and the other two robbers were all dead, this one—it proved the kind of animal he really was—stuffed the money into his pockets and celebrated the event by drinking over their still-bleeding bodies.

The defense argued that Jefferson was innocent of

all charges except being at the wrong place at the wrong time. There was absolutely no proof that there had been a conspiracy between himself and the other two. The fact that Mr. Gropé shot only Brother and Bear was proof of Jefferson's innocence. Why did Mr. Gropé shoot one boy twice and never shoot at Jefferson once? Because Jefferson was merely an innocent bystander. He took the whiskey to calm his nerves, not to celebrate. He took the money out of hunger and plain stupidity.

"Gentlemen of the jury, look at this—this—this boy. I almost said man, but I can't say man. Oh, sure, he has reached the age of twenty-one, when we, civilized men, consider the male species has reached manhood, but would you call this—this—this a man? No, not I. I would call it a boy and a fool. A fool is not aware of right and wrong. A fool does what others tell him to do. A fool got into that automobile. A man with a modicum of intelligence would have seen that those racketeers meant no good. But not a fool. A fool got into that automobile. A fool rode to the grocery store. A fool stood by and watched this happen, not having the sense to run.

"Gentlemen of the jury, look at him—look at him—look at this. Do you see a man sitting here? Do you see a man sitting here? I ask you, I implore, look carefully—do you see a man sitting here? Look at the shape of this skull, this face as flat as the palm of my hand—look deeply into those eyes. Do you see a modicum of intelligence? Do you see anyone here who could plan a murder, a robbery, can plan—can plan—can plan anything? A cornered animal to strike quickly out of fear, a trait inherited from his ancestors in the deepest jungle of blackest Africa—yes, yes, that he can do—but to plan? To plan, gentlemen of the jury? No, gentlemen, this skull here holds no plans. What you see here is a thing that acts on command. A thing to hold the handle of a plow, a thing to load your bales of cotton, a thing to dig your ditches, to chop your wood, to pull your corn. That is what you see here, but you do not see anything capable of planning a robbery or a murder. He does not even know the size of his clothes or his shoes. Ask him to name the months of the year. Ask him does Christmas come before or after the Fourth of July? Mention the names of Keats, Byron, Scott, and see whether the eyes will show one moment of recognition. Ask him to describe a rose, to quote one passage from the Constitution or the Bill of Rights. Gentlemen of the jury, this man planned a robbery? Oh, pardon me, pardon me, I surely did not mean to insult your intelligence by saying 'man'—would you please forgive me for committing such an error?

"Gentlemen of the jury, who would be hurt if you took this life? Look back to that second row. Please look. I want all twelve of you honorable men to turn your heads and look back to that second row. What you see there has been everything to him—mama, grandmother, godmother—everything. Look at her, gentlemen of the jury, look at her well. Take this away from her, and she has no reason to go on living. We may see him as not much, but he's her reason for existence. Think on that, gentlemen, think on it.

"Gentlemen of the jury, be merciful. For God's sake, be merciful. He is innocent of all charges brought against him.

"But let us say he was not. Let us for a moment say he was not. What justice would there be to take this life? Justice, gentlemen? Why, I would just as soon put a hog in the electric chair as this.

"I thank you, gentlemen, from the bottom of my heart, for your kind patience. I have no more to say, except this: We must live with our own conscience. Each and every one of us must live with his own conscience."

The jury retired, and it returned a verdict after lunch: guilty of robbery and murder in the first degree. The judge commended the twelve white men for reaching a quick and just verdict. This was Friday. He would pass sentence on Monday.

Ten o'clock on Monday, Miss Emma and my aunt sat in the same seats they had occupied on Friday. Reverend Mose Ambrose, the pastor of their church, was with them. He and my aunt sat on either side of Miss Emma. The judge, a short, red-faced man with snow-white hair and thick black eyebrows, asked Jefferson if he had anything to say before the sentencing. My aunt said that Jefferson was looking down at the floor and shook his head. The judge told Jefferson that he had been found guilty of the charges brought against him, and that the judge saw no reason that he should not pay for the part he played in this horrible crime.

Death by electrocution. The governor would set the date.

JAMES

BALDWIN

FROM

If Beale Street Could Talk

I MET FONNY IN the streets of this city. I was little, he was not so little. I was around six—somewhere around there—and he was around nine. They lived across the street, him and his family, his mother and two older sisters and his father, and his father ran a tailor shop. Looking back, now, I kind of wonder who he ran the tailor shop *for:* we didn't know anybody who had money to take clothes to the tailor—well, maybe once in a great while. But I don't think *we* could have kept him in business. Of course, as I've been told, people, colored people, weren't as poor then as they had been when my Mama and Daddy were trying to get it together. They weren't as poor then as we had been in the South. But we were certainly poor enough, and we still are.

I never really noticed Fonny until once we got into a fight, after school. This fight didn't really have anything to do with Fonny and me at all. I had a girl friend, named Geneva, a kind of loud, raunchy girl, with her hair plaited tight on her head, with big, ashy knees and long legs and big feet; and she was always into something. Naturally she was my best friend, since I was never into anything. I was skinny and scared and so I followed her and got into all *her* shit. Nobody else wanted me, really, and you *know* that nobody else wanted her. Well, she said that she couldn't stand Fonny. Every time she looked at him, it just made her sick. She was always telling me how ugly he was, with skin just like raw, wet potato rinds and eyes like a Chinaman and all that nappy hair and them thick lips. And so bowlegged he had bunions on his ankle bones; and the way his behind stuck out, his mother must have been a gorilla. I agreed with her because I had to, but I didn't really think he was as bad as all that. I kind of liked his eyes, and, to tell the truth, I thought that if people in China had eyes like that, I wouldn't mind going to China. I had never seen a gorilla, so his behind looked perfectly normal to me, and wasn't, really, when you had to think about it, as big as Geneva's; and it wasn't until much later that I realized that he was, yes, a little bowlegged. But Geneva was always up in Fonny's face. I don't think he ever noticed her at all. He was always too busy with his friends, who were the worst boys on the block. They were always coming down the street, in rags, bleeding, full of lumps, and, just before this fight, Fonny had lost a tooth.

Fonny had a friend named Daniel, a big, black boy,

and Daniel had a thing about Geneva something like the way Geneva had a thing about Fonny. And I don't remember how it all started, but, finally, Daniel had Geneva down on the ground, the two of them rolling around, and I was trying to pull Daniel off her and Fonny was pulling on me. I turned around and hit him with the only thing I could get my hands on, I grabbed it out of the garbage can. It was only a stick; but it had a nail in it. The nail raked across his cheek and it broke the skin and the blood started dripping. I couldn't believe my eyes, I was so scared. Fonny put his hand to his face and then looked at me and then looked at his hand and I didn't have any better sense than to drop the stick and run. Fonny ran after me and, to make matters worse, Geneva saw the blood and she started screaming that I'd killed him, I'd killed him! Fonny caught up to me in no time and he grabbed me tight and he spit at me through the hole where his tooth used to be. He caught me right on the mouth, and—it so *humiliated* me, I guess—because he hadn't hit me, or hurt me—and maybe because I sensed what he had not done—that I screamed and started to cry. It's funny. Maybe my life changed in that very moment when Fonny's spit hit me in the mouth. Geneva and Daniel, who had started the whole thing, and didn't have a scratch on them, both began to scream at me. Geneva said that I'd killed him for sure, yes, I'd killed him, people caught the lockjaw and died from rusty nails. And Daniel said, Yes, he knew, he had a uncle down home who died like that. Fonny was listening to all this, while the blood kept dripping and I kept crying. Finally, he must have realized that they were talking about him, and that he was a dead man—or boy—because he started crying, too, and then Daniel and Geneva took him between them and walked off, leaving me there, alone.

And I didn't see Fonny for a couple of days. I was sure he had the lockjaw, and was dying; and Geneva said that just as soon as he was dead, which would be any minute, the police would come and put me in the electric chair. I watched the tailor shop, but everything seemed normal. Mr. Hunt was there, with his laughing, light-brown-skinned self, pressing pants, and telling jokes to whoever was in the shop—there was always someone in the shop—and every once in a while, Mrs. Hunt would come by. She was a Sanctified woman, who didn't smile much, but, still, neither of them acted as if their son was dying.

So, when I hadn't seen Fonny for a couple of days, I waited until the tailor shop seemed empty, when Mr. Hunt was in there by himself, and I went over there. Mr. Hunt knew me, then, a little, like we all knew each other on the block.

"Hey, Tish," he said, "how you doing? How's the family?"

I said, "Just fine, Mr. Hunt." I wanted to say, How's *your* family? which I always *did* say and had planned to say, but I couldn't.

"How you doing in school?" he asked me, after

a minute: and I thought he looked at me in a real strange way.

"Oh, all right," I said, and my heart started to beating like it was going to jump out of my chest.

Mr. Hunt pressed down that sort of double ironing board they have in tailor shops—like two ironing boards facing each other—he pressed that down, and he looked at me for a minute and then he laughed and said, "Reckon that big-headed boy of mine be back here pretty soon."

I heard what he said, and I understood—something; but I didn't know what it was I understood.

I walked to the door of the shop, making like I was going out, and then I turned and I said, "What's that, Mr. Hunt?"

Mr. Hunt was still smiling. He pulled the presser down and turned over the pants or whatever it was he had in there, and said, "Fonny. His Mama sent him down to her folks in the country for a little while. Claim he get into too much trouble up here."

He pressed the presser down again. "She don't know what kind of trouble he like to get in down there." Then he looked up at me and he smiled. When I got to know Fonny and I got to know Mr. Hunt better, I realized that Fonny has his smile. "Oh, I'll tell him you come by," he said.

I said, "Say hello to the family for me, Mr. Hunt," and I ran across the street.

Geneva was on my stoop and she told me I looked like a fool and that I'd almost got run over.

I stopped and said, "You a liar, Geneva Braithwaite. Fonny ain't got the lockjaw and he ain't going to die. And I ain't going to jail. Now, you just go and ask his Daddy." And then Geneva gave me such a funny look that I ran up my stoop and up the stairs and I sat down on the fire escape, but sort of in the window, where she couldn't see me.

Fonny came back, about four or five days later, and he came over to my stoop. He didn't have a scar on him. He had two doughnuts. He sat down on my stoop. He said, "I'm sorry I spit in your face." And he gave me one of his doughnuts.

I said, "I'm sorry I hit you." And then we didn't say anything. He ate his doughnut and I ate mine.

People don't believe it about boys and girls that age—people don't believe much and I'm beginning to know why—but, then, we got to be friends. Or, maybe, and it's really the same thing—something else people don't want to know—I got to be his little sister and he got to be my big brother. He didn't like his sisters and I didn't have any brothers. And so we got to be, for each other, what the other missed.

Geneva got mad at me and she stopped being my friend; though, maybe, now that I think about it, without even knowing it, I stopped being *her* friend; because, now—and without knowing what that meant—I had Fonny. Daniel got mad at Fonny, he called him a sissy for fooling around with girls, and he stopped being Fonny's friend—for a long time; they even had a fight and Fonny lost another tooth. I think that anyone watching Fonny then was sure that he'd grow up without a single tooth in his head. I remember telling Fonny that I'd get my mother's scissors from upstairs and go and kill Daniel, but Fonny said I wasn't nothing but a girl and didn't have nothing to do with it.

Fonny had to go to church on Sundays—and I mean, he *had* to go: though he managed to outwit his mother more often than she knew, or cared to know. His mother—I got to know her better, too, later on, and we're going to talk about her in a minute—was, as I've said, a Sanctified woman and if she couldn't save her husband, she was damn sure going to save her child. Because it was *her* child; it wasn't *their* child.

I think that's why Fonny was so bad. And I think that's why he was, when you got to know him, so nice, a really nice person, a really sweet man, with something very sad in him: when you got to know him. Mr. Hunt, Frank, didn't try to claim him but he loved him—loves him. The two older sisters weren't Sanctified exactly, but they might as well have been, and they certainly took after their mother. So that left just Frank and Fonny. In a way, Frank had Fonny all week long, Fonny had Frank all week long. They both knew this and that was why Frank could give Fonny to his mother on Sundays. What Fonny was doing in the street was just exactly what Frank was doing in the tailor shop and in the house. He was being bad. That's why he hold on to that tailor shop as long as he could. That's why, when Fonny came home bleeding, Frank could tend to him; that's why they could, both the father and the son, love me. It's not really a mystery except it's always a mystery about people. I used to wonder, later, if Fonny's mother and father ever made love together. I asked Fonny. And Fonny said:

"Yeah. But not like you and me. I used to hear them. She'd come home from church, wringing wet and funky. She'd act like she was so tired she could hardly move and she'd just fall across the bed with her clothes on—she'd maybe had enough strength to take off her shoes. And her hat. And she'd always lay her handbag down someplace. I can still hear that sound, like something heavy, with silver inside it, dropping heavy wherever she laid it down. I'd hear her say, The Lord sure blessed my soul this evening. Honey, when you going to give your life to the Lord? And, baby, he'd say, and I swear to you he was lying there with his dick getting hard, and, excuse me, baby, but her condition weren't no better, because this, you dig? was like the game you hear two alley cats playing in the alley. Shit. She going to whelp and *mee-e-ow* till times get better, she going to get that cat, she going to run him all *over* the alley, she going run him till he bite her by the neck—by this time he just want to get some sleep really, but she got her chorus going, he's got to stop the music and ain't but one way to do it—he going to bite her by the neck and then she got him. So, my Daddy just lay there, didn't have no clothes on, with his dick getting harder and harder, and my Daddy would say, About the time, I reckon, that the Lord gives *his* life to *me*. And she'd say, Oh, Frank, let me bring you to the Lord. And he'd say, Shit, woman, I'm going to bring the Lord to *you*. *I'm* the Lord. And she'd start to crying, and she'd moan, Lord, help me help this man. You give him to me. I can't do nothing about it. Oh, Lord, help me. And he'd say, The Lord's going to help you, sugar, just as soon as you get to be a little child again, naked, like a little child. Come on, come to the Lord. And she'd start to crying and calling on Jesus while he started taking all her clothes off—I could hear them kind of rustling and whistling and tearing and falling to the floor and sometimes I'd get my foot caught in one of them things when I was coming through their room in the morning on my way to school—and when he got her naked and got on top of her and she was still crying, Jesus! help me, Lord! my Daddy would say, You got the Lord now, right here. Where you want your blessing? Where do it hurt? Where you want the Lord's hands to touch you? here? here? or here? Where you want his tongue? Where you want the Lord to enter you, you dirty, dumb black bitch? you bitch. You bitch. You bitch. And he'd slap her, hard, loud. And she'd say, Oh, Lord, help me to bear my burden. And he'd say, Here it is, baby, you going to bear it all right, I know it. You got a friend in Jesus, and I'm going to tell you when he comes. The first time. We don't know nothing about the second coming. Yet. And the bed would shake and she would moan and moan and moan. And, in the morning, was just like nothing never happened. She was just like she had been. She still belonged to Jesus and he went off down the street, to the shop."

And then Fonny said, "Hadn't been for me, I believe the cat would have split the scene. I'll always love my Daddy because he didn't leave me." I'll always remember Fonny's face when he talked about his Daddy.

Then, Fonny would turn to me and take me in his arms and laugh and say, "You remind me a lot of my mother, you know that? Come on, now, and let's sing together, Sinner, do you love my Lord?—And if I don't hear no moaning, I'll know you ain't been saved."

I guess it can't be too often that two people can laugh and make love, too, make love because they are laughing, laugh because they're making love. The love and the laughter come from the same place: but not many people go there.

ROSA

GUY

FROM

The Friends

1.

HER NAME WAS EDITH.

I did not like her. Edith always came to school with her clothes unpressed, her stockings bagging about her legs with big holes, which she tried to hide by pulling them into her shoes but which kept slipping up, on each heel, to expose a round, brown circle of dry skin the size of a quarter. Of course there were many children in this class that were untidy and whom I did not like. Some were tough. So tough that I was afraid of them. But at least they did not have to sit right across the aisle from me. Nor did they try to be friendly as Edith did—whenever she happened to come to school.

Edith walked into the classroom at late morning, causing the teacher to stop in the middle of one of her monotonous sentences to fasten a hate-filled glare, which Edith never saw, on her back.

"Good afternoon, Miss Jackson," the teacher's voice,

thick with sarcasm, followed her to her seat. But Edith, popping bubble gum on her back teeth so that it distorted her square little face, slammed her books on the desk, slipped her wiry body into her seat, then turned her head around the room nodding greetings to friends.

The teacher's voice rose sharply: "It seems to me that if you *had* to honor us with your presence today, you could at least have been preparing yourself to come to class looking presentable."

Her words had more effect on the class than on Edith. They always did. When I had first come into class I had thought it was because the teacher was white. Later I realized that it was because of the manner she spoke to the pupils. Now, the shuffle of feet sounded around the room, a banging of desks. The teacher shrilled: "I am talking to you, Edith Jackson."

"Huh, what?—oh, you talking to me? Good afternoon, Miss Lass." Edith grinned with open-faced innocence. The teacher reddened. Edith turned her impish grin to include all of the appreciative snickers around the room. She then leaned across the aisle and said to me: "Hi ya doin', Phyllisia?"

I pulled myself tall in my seat, made haughty little movements with my shoulders and head, adjusted the frills on the collar of my well-ironed blouse, touched my soft, neatly plaited hair and pointedly gave my attention to the blackboard.

Edith ignored my snub. She always ignored my

snubs. Edith had made up her mind, from the first day I entered this class, that she would be my friend whether I wanted it or not. "Ain't it a pretty day out?" She grinned and made a loud explosion with her gum. "Sure hated to come and stick myself in this dingy-ass classroom."

Her words pulled my attention away from the blackboard and to the window where the sun came splashing into the room.

Since my father had sent for us, my sister Ruby who is sixteen and me, two years younger, and set us down in this miserable place called Harlem, New York, this was the first warm day. I, too, had not wanted to come here today. Walking to school, seeing people coming out of their homes with faces softened by smiles, for the first time I had been filled with the desire to run off somewhere, anywhere but to this room. I had not wanted to have to listen to a teacher I did not like, nor to sit among children I liked even less. But where could I go? I knew nothing about this strange city. Going one block out of my way between home and school, and I would be lost. And so I had come, grudgingly, but I had come.

Yet the moment I had entered the classroom, I knew that my instincts had been right. I should not have come today. The same recklessness that had pulled at me in the streets was big in the room, pulling and tugging at the control of the students. Fear cut a zig-zag pattern from my stomach to my chest: The students in the class did not like *me*.

They mocked my West Indian accent, called me names—"monkey" was one of the nicer ones. Sometimes they waited after school to tease me, following me at times for several blocks, shouting. But it had been cold and after a time they had been only too glad to hunch their shoulders up to their ears and go home. Winter, as much as I hated it, had protected me. Now it was spring.

Automatically my gaze sought the big-breasted girl sitting diagonally across the room from me—Beulah. Beulah sat with her head bowed down to the desk obviously reading a comic book she had concealed beneath. Beulah was the toughest girl I had ever known. She was so tough that she did anything she wanted to in class, and Miss Lass looked the other way. But the worst of it was that Beulah for some reason *hated* me.

"Come on, let's split this scene," Edith whispered. "I got money. We can go to some jazzy place and wait the time out."

Her words lit my mind with pictures of what she meant by jazzy places—places like parks and lakes and outdoor movies. All I had to do was turn and smile at this dirty little girl and she could take me to places that I had never been to before. But then I thought about Calvin and the brilliant thoughts fizzled out.

Calvin is my father. To myself I use his first name, as a sign of disrespect. The first week we had come, I demanded of him why he had sent for us to set us down in this trap of asphalt and stone called Harlem.

"Because I have the right. To control your rudeness better," he had said. "What blame control does he think we need," I had muttered to my sister Ruby loud enough for him to hear. The next moment my lips were swelling up from a backhand slap. I had not even seen it coming. "*Who* needs control?" he asked. I sulked at first, refusing to answer. But the next time he said, "I ask you, who needs control?" I gave one look into his set, black face, with anger burning out of his eyes, and my determination not to answer flickered out. "Me," I answered meekly, and my hatred of him mounted.

No, it would not do for Calvin to see me out in the streets when I should be in school. And with someone looking like Edith?

I pulled my attention back into the room just in time to hear Miss Lass throw a question in my direction.

"Can anyone tell me on what continent the country of Egypt is located?" she asked.

I stared fixedly at the blackboard. While it was certain I could not leave school, it was also certain that I did not feel like standing in the full glare of the children's animosity on this warm touchy day to answer any questions.

Teacher waited. The class waited. I waited, praying someone else would know the answer and, barring that, Miss Lass herself would explain. I did not remember her ever discussing Africa before. But I had been the star pupil too long—always jumping up to let others know how smart I was. And so Miss Lass kept looking at me while I kept looking at the blackboard. Finally, after a few minutes, she called: "Phyllisia?"

I did not move. Why did she want to make an example of me to the other children? There were at least thirty others she could call on. "Phyllisia!" I still kept my seat. I kept repeating to myself: I will not stand. I will not answer. I will not.

Then someone snickered, and someone else. My face burned with shame. Sitting there and not answering was like begging. And why should I beg? I had done nothing to anybody. I found myself standing. I heard my voice saying, despite a sixth sense warning me to remain silent, to stay in my seat, "Egypt is in Africa." Once started I kept on talking to dispel any notion that I might be guessing. "It is bordered on the South by the Sudan and on the North by the Mediterranean Sea which opens up into the Nile, which is the longest river in Africa and perhaps the world."

I resumed my seat, a taste of chalk in my mouth, unsatisfied with the display of my brilliance. Nor did I feel any better at the flurry of shuffling feet, the banging of more desks and the sound of contemptuous whispers.

"No it ain't either," a boy shouted from the back of the room. "They got A-rabs in Egypt. Everybody know ain't no A-rabs in Africa."

"That's where you are wrong," Miss Lass shrilled. "Egypt *is* a country in Africa. If some of you would follow Phyllisia's example and study your books, then perhaps the intelligence rate in this room might zoom up to zero."

Silently I groaned. Miss Lass had to know better. She had to know that she was setting me up as a target. Any fool would feel the agitation in the room. But that was exactly what she wanted!

I knew it suddenly. Standing in front of the room, her blond hair pulled back to emphasize the determination of her face, her body girdled to emphasize the determination of her spine, her eyes holding determinedly to anger, *Miss Lass was afraid!!* She was afraid and she was using *me* to keep the hatred of the children away from *her*. I was the natural choice because I was a stranger and because I was proud.

The thought seemed to be so loud that it drew her attention, and for one moment we stared startled into each other's eyes. Her face turned a beet red and she shifted her gaze.

I felt a dozen needles sticking in my stomach. I leaned back in my seat. The fingernails of the girl behind me dug into my back. "Teacher's pet," she hissed. I pulled away, but as I did my head magnetically turned and I found myself staring into the eyes of the thick-muscled girl with the breasts. She had turned completely around in her seat so that her back faced the teacher while she stared at me. As our stares locked, she balled up her fist, put it first over one eye and then the other. The needles in my stomach multiplied by thousands.

But Edith, unaware of anything unnatural happening, leaned across the aisle, her eyes wide with admiration. "Girl, you sure are smart. I bet ain't nothing your folks don't teach you, 'cause you sure ain't learned them things in here."

Relieved to break the belligerent stare, I turned, but remembered *who* had spoken, in time to check my gratitude with a stiff nod. Still my heart was thumping. I had to keep telling myself that it was, after all, only the first period. By the end of the day things had to settle back to normal. So I waited anxiously for the bell to signal the end of the period and the change of class.

2.

By the last period what had started out as a mild spring day flourished into full summer heat. The children, shouting and screaming, came charging back into their homeroom. The discipline established during winter at the expense of the teacher's good disposition had been washed away by the sudden warmth. It took the last bit of Miss Lass's energy to maintain shoestring control as we waited for the final bell.

I did not want the bell to ring. All of the pupils' restlessness, their resentment over their senseless imprisonment on this overripe day, seemed directed toward me, as well as the serpentine stare that big-breasted Beulah kept burning at the side of my face. I did not want to leave the classroom. Tempted to ask Miss Lass to let me stay to help with chores after school, I changed my mind at the look of her face shiny from sweat, with its lips gone along with her lipstick, the escaped strands of blond hair hanging limply over her angular face—her look of aching wickedness.

I had waited for Edith.

Edith had not come in with the rest of the class. She never did. Teacher called her a straggler. Today when she straggled in from her last class I intended to surprise her. I was going to smile and make friends with her. At one time during the day I had reasoned that the children singled me out for abuse because I walked alone. They might leave me in peace if I walked with a friend. And so I had sat staring at the door waiting for the one girl I could use, my heart giving little leaps of delight everytime someone entered, and sinking in dismay—almost down to my stomach—when it was not Edith.

Soon, however, I had accepted the obvious. Edith had carried out her earlier promise and had ducked out of school as the weather grew warmer. Now I wanted to leave too, panicky at the feeling of violence around me. If I were just to get up and go, start running, I could be far away from the school before class was dismissed. But gathering enough courage to simply walk out was not easy, and between the thought and the moment to act the bell rang, and the class made their dash for freedom.

A crowd was waiting for me when I walked down the

outside steps of the school. They had gathered as though the entire school had been given notice that a rumble was on. Leaving no doubt that I was the intended victim, a bloody roar rose when I appeared on the steps.

Glancing through the crowd with pretended casualness, I picked out some of my classmates. Most were standing in front, with big-breasted Beulah first, her evil intentions plastered over her face. The thin girl who had dug her fingernails in my back stood behind her, whispering excitedly in her ear.

On stoops around the school and across the street, grownups stood looking at the yelling mob. At windows of buildings more adults adjusted themselves to get a better view. Was there one who might come down to help a young girl, desperate with fear, ready to be set upon by a mob? I knew the answer. No.

My pride was crumbling. To preserve some of it, I had to move quickly. So, holding my book bag tightly to my chest, I stuck my head up, walked down the steps and pushed boldly past Beulah, with her big breasts pushed aggressively out.

But my back quivered as I passed as though it had eyes and actually did see the powerful hands reach out and push me. Push me toward a little boy who stepped cunningly out of my way. And there I was face to face with the girl who sat behind me in class.

This girl was tall and as thin as I. I knew I could match her strength. But what if I started to fight her and Beulah jumped in too? While trying to make up my mind, the thin girl quickly shoved me back into the waiting leathery arms of the girl I feared the most.

"You dirty West Indian," she hissed in my ear. "You ain't rapping so big out here, is you? No, you ain't rapping so big out here. We should get Miss Lassy-assy out so she can see how you ain't doing no big-time talking and acting better than anybody."

"West Indian?" A boy called out. "My Ma call them monkey chasers."

"Monkey chaser, monkey chaser, bring monkey soup for your monkey father."

Someone else shouted in a mock West Indian accent: "Run her into the sea, mahn. What she want here nohow? We ain't got no trees to swing from."

My dry tongue licked drier lips, my knees buckled as I tried once again to push through the dense crowd. Blocking my way was a boy who stuck his hand under my chin. "Best man hit this." It was their idea of fair play: If I was a "good sport," I would hit the boy's hand, the boy would then hit Beulah, who would complete the cycle by hitting me to start the fight.

I pretended I did not see the hand.

"West Indian ain't gonna hit shit," Beulah sneered. "I'll hit it." She hit the hand. The hand in turn hit me. I was now supposed to hit Beulah to complete the cycle. My body quaked. I clutched my book bag to my chest and again tried to shoulder my way through.

"Pardon me," I said, forcing politeness. "I . . ."

"Dig that rap," the thin girl jeered. "Pardon me. Who the hell she think she is?"

"Always trying to act better than the folks," Beulah sneered. Then with her thick, strong hands she spun me around punching her fist against my nose. "Don't push me," she yelled at the same time. "You see she pushed me?" Not expecting any answer she kept on punching and punching.

Blood ran from my nose and I tasted more in my mouth. I encircled my head with my arms. A blow caught me in my ribs. I doubled over, put my book bag to protect my stomach, and the fists pounded my face again.

"Old Big-Tits sure can fight."

"Yeah. She gonna smash that monkey into a African monkey stew."

I crouched trying to arouse pity. If not in the children, certainly in some of the grownups looking on. That was a mistake. At my look of utter helplessness the children jeered. "Let's finish her off," someone yelled. They moved in around me.

In terror I leveled my head, rammed it in the direction of the jabbing fists. It contacted with the fleshy chest. The girl staggered. I backed up, rammed forward again. This time the thick, tough girl sprawled backwards to the sidewalk and lay there squirming in pain. I ran over her, kicked her face out of the way of my flying feet, hit the person in front of me with my shoulder—the crowd opened up and I ran for my life.

I did not feel the ground beneath my feet nor see the street crossings. I heard horns blowing, brakes screeching, blending with the jeers which seemed a very part of the air that I was so painfully breathing. Clouds of fear came and went carrying me for blocks before I realized that no one was following me. By that time, exhausted, unable to run further, I leaned against the iron rail of an apartment building, holding my sides and gasping for breath.

"Oh God, I hate those kids," I muttered. "I hate them. I hate them." Tears came, and I wiped them from my eyes and the blood from my nose with one sweep of my arm. I examined my face with my fingers, touched my thickened lips, the swelling that stretched my skin smooth, hiding the dividing lines that separated nose from cheeks, then tears came again.

Walking slowly, painfully toward my street, I stared hard into the faces of grownups, searching for a look of pity, of concern, wishing just one person would ask me: "What happened, little girl?" Then I could explain to somebody, and they might tell me what I was doing wrong. Why nobody liked me. But no older person stopped to look at me or to ask me. They just did not notice me.

TONI CADE

BAMBARA

Gorilla, My Love

THAT WAS THE YEAR Hunca Bubba changed his name. Not a change up, but a change back, since Jefferson Winston Vale was the name in the first place. Which was news to me cause he'd been my Hunca Bubba my whole lifetime, since I couldn't manage Uncle to save my life. So far as I was concerned it was a change completely to somethin soundin very geographical weatherlike to me, like somethin you'd find in a almanac. Or somethin you'd run across when you sittin in the navigator seat with a wet thumb on the map crinkly in your lap, watchin the roads and signs so when Granddaddy Vale say "Which way, Scout," you got sense enough to say take the next exit or take a left or whatever it is. Not that Scout's my name. Just the name Granddaddy call whoever sittin in the navigator seat. Which is usually me cause I don't feature sittin in the back with the pecans. Now, you figure pecans all right to be sittin with. If you thinks so, that's your business. But they dusty sometime and make you cough.

And they got a way of slidin around and dippin down sudden, like maybe a rat in the buckets. So if you scary like me, you sleep with the lights on and blame it on Baby Jason and, so as not to waste good electric, you study the maps. And that's how come I'm in the navigator seat most times and get to be called Scout.

So Hunca Bubba in the back with the pecans and Baby Jason, and he in love. And we got to hear all this stuff about this woman he in love with and all. Which really ain't enough to keep the mind alive, though Baby Jason got no better sense than to give his undivided attention and keep grabbin at the photograph which is just a picture of some skinny woman in a countrified dress with her hand shot up to her face like she shame fore cameras. But there's a movie house in the background which I ax about. Cause I am a movie freak from way back, even though it do get me in trouble sometime.

Like when me and Big Brood and Baby Jason was on our own last Easter and couldn't go to the Dorset cause we'd seen all the Three Stooges they was. And the RKO Hamilton was closed readying up for the Easter Pageant that night. And the West End, the Regun, and the Sunset was too far, less we had grownups with us which we didn't. So we walk up Amsterdam Avenue to the Washington and *Gorilla, My Love* playin, they say, which suit me just fine, though the "my love" part kinda drag Big Brood some. As for Baby Jason, shoot, like Granddaddy say, he'd follow me into the fiery furnace if I say come on. So we go in and get three bags of Havmore potato chips which not only are the best potato chips but the best bags for blowin up and bustin real loud so the matron come trottin down the aisle with her chunky self, flashin that flashlight dead in your eye so you can give her some lip, and if she answer back and you already finish seein the show anyway, why then you just turn the place out. Which I love to do, no lie. With Baby Jason kickin at the seat in front, egging me on, and Big Brood mumblin bout what fiercesome things we goin do. Which means me. Like when the big boys come up on us talkin bout Lemme a nickel. It's me that hide the money. Or when the bad boys in the park take Big Brood's Spaudeen way from him. It's me that jump on they back and fight awhile. And it's me that turns out the show if the matron get too salty.

So the movie come on and right away it's this churchy music and clearly not about no gorilla. Bout Jesus. And I am ready to kill, not cause I got anything gainst Jesus. Just that when you fixed to watch a gorilla picture you don't wanna get messed around with Sunday School stuff. So I am mad. Besides, we see this raggedy old brown film *King of Kings* every year and enough's enough. Grownups figure they can treat you just anyhow. Which burns me up. There I am, my feet up and my Havmore potato chips really salty and crispy and two jawbreakers in my lap and the money safe in my shoe from the big boys, and here comes this Jesus stuff. So we all go wild. Yellin, booin, stompin, and carryin on. Really to wake the man in the booth up there who musta went to sleep and put on the wrong reels. But no, cause he holler down to shut up and then he turn the sound up so we really gotta holler like crazy to even hear ourselves good. And the matron ropes off the children section and flashes her light all over the place and we yell some more and some kids slip under the rope and run up and down the aisle just to show it take more than some dusty ole velvet rope to tie us down. And I'm flingin the kid in front of me's popcorn. And Baby Jason kickin seats. And it's really somethin. Then here comes the big and bad matron, the one they let out in case of emergency. And she totin that flashlight like she gonna use it on somebody. This here the colored matron Brandy and her friends call Thunderbuns. She do not play. She do not smile. So we shut up and watch the simple ass picture.

Which is not so simple as it is stupid. Cause I realize that just about anybody in my family is better than this god they always talkin about. My Daddy wouldn't stand for nobody treatin any of us that way. My Mama specially. And I can just see it now, Big Brood up there on the cross talkin bout Forgive them Daddy cause they don't know what they doin. And my Mama say Get on down from there you big fool, whatcha think this is, playtime? And my Daddy yellin to Granddaddy to get him a ladder cause Big Brood actin the fool, his mother side of the family showin up. And my Mama and her sister Daisy jumpin on them Romans beatin them with they pocketbooks. And Hunca Bubba tellin them folks on they knees they better get out the way and go get some help or they goin to get trampled on. And Granddaddy Vale sayin Leave the boy alone, if that's what he wants to do with his life we ain't got nothin to say about it. Then Aunt Daisy givin him a taste of that pocketbook, fussin bout what a damn fool old man Granddaddy is. Then everybody jumpin in his chest like the time Uncle Clayton went in the army and come back with only one leg and Granddaddy say somethin stupid about that's life. And by this time Big Brood off the cross and in the park playin handball or skully or somethin. And the family in the kitchen throwin dishes at each other, screamin bout if you hadn't done this I wouldn't had to do that. And me in the parlor trying to do my arithmetic yellin Shut it off.

Which is what I was yellin all by myself which make me a sittin target for Thunderbuns. But when I yell We want our money back, that gets everybody in chorus. And the movie windin up with this heavenly cloud music and the smart-ass up there in his hole in the wall turns up the sound again to drown us out. Then there comes Bugs Bunny which we already seen so we know we been had. No gorilla my nuthin. And Big Brood say Awwww sheeet, we goin to see the manager and get our money back. And I know from this we business. So I brush the potato chips out of my hair which is where Baby Jason likes to put em, and I march myself up the aisle to deal with the manager who is a crook in the first place for lyin out there sayin *Gorilla, My Love* playin. And I never did like the man cause he oily and pasty at the same time like the bad guy in the serial, the one that got a hideout behind a push-button bookcase and play "Moonlight Sonata" with gloves on. I knock on the door and I am furious. And I am alone, too. Cause Big Brood suddenly got to go so bad even though my Mama told us bout goin in them nasty bathrooms. And I hear him sigh like he disgusted when he get to the door and see only a little kid there. And now I'm really furious cause I get so tired grownups messin over kids just cause they little and can't take em to court. What is it, he say to me like I lost my mittens or wet on myself or am somebody's retarded child. When in reality I am the smartest kid P.S. 186 ever had in its whole lifetime and you can ax anybody. Even them teachers that don't like me cause I won't sing them Southern songs or back off when they tell me my questions are out of order. And cause my Mama come up there in a minute when them teachers start playin the dozens behind colored folks. She stalk in with her hat pulled down bad and that Persian lamb coat draped back over one hip on account of she got her fist planted there so she can talk that talk which gets us all hypnotized, and teacher be comin undone cause she know this could be her job and her behind cause Mama got pull with the Board and bad by her own self anyhow.

So I kick the door open wider and just walk right by

him and sit down and tell the man about himself and that I want my money back and that goes for Baby Jason and Big Brood too. And he still trying to shuffle me out the door even though I'm sittin which shows him for the fool he is. Just like them teachers do fore they realize Mama like a stone on that spot and ain't backin up. So he ain't gettin up off the money. So I was forced to leave, takin the matches from under his ashtray, and set a fire under the candy stand, which closed the raggedy ole Washington down for a week. My Daddy had the suspect it was me cause Big Brood got a big mouth. But I explained right quick what the whole thing was about and I figured it was even-steven. Cause if you say Gorilla, My Love, you suppose to mean it. Just like when you say you goin to give me a party on my birthday, you gotta mean it. And if you say me and Baby Jason can go South pecan haulin with Granddaddy Vale, you better not be comin up with no stuff about the weather look uncertain or did you mop the bathroom or any other trickified business. I mean even gangsters in the movies say My word is my bond. So don't nobody get away with nothin far as I'm concerned. So Daddy put his belt back on. Cause that's the way I was raised. Like my Mama say in one of them situations when I won't back down, Okay Badbird, you right. Your point is well-taken. Not that Badbird my name, just what she say when she tired arguin and know I'm right. And Aunt Jo, who is the hardest head in the family and worse even than Aunt Daisy, she say,

You absolutely right Miss Muffin, which also ain't my real name but the name she gave me one time when I got some medicine shot in my behind and wouldn't get up off her pillows for nothin. And even Granddaddy Vale—who got no memory to speak of, so sometime you can just plain lie to him, if you want to be like that—he say, Well if that's what I said, then that's it. But this name business was different they said. It wasn't like Hunca Bubba had gone back on his word or anything. Just that he was thinkin bout gettin married and was usin his real name now. Which ain't the way I saw it at all.

So there I am in the navigator seat. And I turn to him and just plain ole ax him. I mean I come right on out with it. No sense goin all around that barn the old folks talk about. And like my Mama say, Hazel—which is my real name and what she remembers to call me when she bein serious—when you got somethin on your mind, speak up and let the chips fall where they may. And if anybody don't like it, tell em to come see your Mama. And Daddy look up from the paper and say, You hear your Mama good, Hazel. And tell em to come see me first. Like that. That's how I was raised.

So I turn clear round in the navigator seat and say, "Look here, Hunca Bubba or Jefferson Windsong Vale or whatever your name is, you gonna marry this girl?"

"Sure am," he say, all grins.

And I say, "Member that time you was baby-sittin me when we lived at four-o-nine and there was this big snow and Mama and Daddy got held up in the country so you had to stay for two days?"

And he say, "Sure do."

"Well. You remember how you told me I was the cutest thing that ever walked the earth?"

"Oh, you were real cute when you were little," he say, which is suppose to be funny. I am not laughin.

"Well. You remember what you said?"

And Granddaddy Vale squintin over the wheel and axin Which way, Scout. But Scout is busy and don't care if we all get lost for days.

"Watcha mean, Peaches?"

"My name is Hazel. And what I mean is you said you were going to marry *me* when I grew up. You were going to wait. That's what I mean, my dear Uncle Jefferson." And he don't say nuthin. Just look at me real strange like he never saw me before in life. Like he lost in some weird town in the middle of night and lookin for directions and there's no one to ask. Like it was me that messed up the maps and turned the road posts round. "Well, you said it, didn't you?" And Baby Jason lookin back and forth like we playin ping-pong. Only I ain't playin. I'm hurtin and I can hear that I am screamin. And Granddaddy Vale mumblin how we never gonna get to where we goin if I don't turn around and take my navigator job serious.

"Well, for cryin out loud, Hazel, you just a little girl. And I was just teasin."

" 'And I was just teasin,' " I say back just how he said

it so he can hear what a terrible thing it is. Then I don't say nuthin. And he don't say nuthin. And Baby Jason don't say nuthin nohow. Then Granddaddy Vale speak up. "Look here, Precious, it was Hunca Bubba what told you them things. This here, Jefferson Winston Vale." And Hunca Bubba say, "That's right. That was somebody else. I'm a new somebody."

"You a lyin dawg," I say, when I meant to say treacherous dog, but just couldn't get hold of the word. It slipped away from me. And I'm crying and crumplin down in the seat and just don't care. And Granddaddy say to hush and steps on the gas. And I'm losin my bearins and don't even know where to look on the map cause I can't see for cryin. And Baby Jason cryin too. Cause he is my blood brother and understands that we must stick together or be forever lost, what with grownups playin change-up and turnin you round every which way so bad. And don't even say they sorry.

TIM

SEIBLES

Latin

Words slip into a language the way
white-green shoots slide between slats in a fence.

A couple opens the door to a restaurant,
sees the orange and black colors everywhere

and the waitress grins, "Yeah,
a little Halloween overkill, huh."

Overkill, a noun for all of us
fidgeting under the nuclear umbrella—

but for that instant it just meant too many decorations,
too many paper skeletons and hobgobbled balloons.

I know a woman who is tall with dark hair,
who makes me think of honeysuckle

whenever she opens her legs. Not just the flower
but the dew-soaked music itself *honeysuckle* like a
flavor.

And I remember the first time years back
when LaTina told me what it was we had

between our eight-year-old front teeth
that April afternoon, our hands wet

with rain from the vines. "Honey sickle," she said,
while the white flower bloomed from the side of her
mouth,

and I had a new sweetness on my tongue and
a word
I'd never heard before. How was it decided in the
beginning?

This word for *this* particular thing,
a sound attached to a shape or a feeling forever.

All summer long the cicadas don't know
what we call them.

They sneak from the ground every year after dark,
break out of their shells right into the language,

and it holds them like a net made of nothing
but the need to make everything familiar.

All summer long they rattle trees like maracas
until they become part of our weather—

quiet in rain, crazy in hard sun,
so we say *those cicadas sure make enough noise, huh.*

And the noise of that sentence heard ten-thousand
  times
becomes a name for *us* the cicadas keep trying to say.

I think about dying sometimes,
not the sudden death in the movies—

the red hole in the shirt, the eyes
open like magazines left on a waiting room table—

not that, but withering slowly like a language,
barely holding on until everything

I ever did or said   is just gone, absorbed
into something I would never have imagined—

like Latin. Not lost completely, but moved away
from that bright, small place

between seeing   and naming,
between the slow roll of ocean

and the quick intake of air
that will fill the word *wave*.

PAUL

BEATTY

Big Bowls of Cereal

with absolutely no regrets
i spent the summer of my discontent
in the corner arcade

bent over the pinball machine
nine extra balls and a line of niggas
                                        sucking they teeth
                                        waitin for me to get off

      the change guy thinks i am a genius
      my high scores blink on the backglass
      of every video game ever made

            but my real teenage wasteland claim to fame
            is that every fall i get teased and taunted
            for being the dumbest kid in gifted class

the ultimate idiot savant
i can recite Immanuel Kants *Critique of Pure Reason*
but i cant tell you what "categorical imperative" means

all his grief
cause during an iq test
i strung a string of beads
tossed around some proverbs

when the proctor said
a stitch in time saves nine
i didnt ask nine what   i simply nodded my head
yes   that maxim is the shit

you should have heard me make up the meanings for
the long words
astutely point out the absurd

if the sun sets in the west
how can a tree cast a shadow in that direction

i can give you the day of the week and the weather
for any date in history

the crucifixion?   it was a friday   hazy partly cloudy
with easterly winds

supposedly got a head on my shoulders
but nobody asks me
what i think
only what i know
which isnt much
dont seem to have the scholastic touch

D in trig
slept through college prep

flunked chem
by letting the rules slide
and pass me by

never did memorize all the elements
just sat there
an inert black gas
chemically unreactive to the difference between
density and mass

i was cool with the conversion from celsius to
fahrenheit
but then cuz started talkin about water was thicker
than ice
and i wuz like right

may i be excused from the atomic table

Krypton
Xenon
Neon everyone knows im just a C minus peon
with the dirtiest workstation

unable to balance the electrons in this nuclear age
equation
and according to my calculations

ive come of age
in an age
where age aint nothing but a number

ever since i was ten
i aint never been nothin but a man

yes ma'ams   calloused hands
whats happenin little man

aging faster than a vampire
with a stake in its heart

terrible two
teething on the universe
already old enough
to know better

before i had ever written a love letter
if someones older sister
called my poker faced
peach fuzz
sexual bluff
and asked me how old i was
i knew to say that i was always   old
enough

i am old
old enough to remember shag carpeting

and the matted down path that went from the front
door straight to the bathroom
old enough to remember slow gliding fives on the
black hand side
hip huggers
'n punch bugs 'n free love

old enough to remember when The Gap
was the bogus clothing equivalent of Radio Shack

old enough to know that not knowing whats right
has made me unsure nervous
the type of cat who needs instant feedback

i feel like im always on tv and dont know what to do
with my hands
with every "yo and hello"
my hands move around uncontrollably
the ginsu knives of my mind
slicing and dicing life down to julienne potato size
i feel like i must act now

im a $19.95 plus shipping and handling
type nigga
who everytime he makes a point
taps you on your joints   shoulder   knee
punctuates his speech with rhetorical self-esteem
know whut um sayin
just to see if you're listenin
know whut um sayin

periodically i kick sonic *bust it booms*
not to see if you're moved
but just so it feels like im groovin

so buss it boom

thats me   an ungroomed
                    black boy polaroid
                          underdeveloped grapevine double
                              print of my dad
being driven mad by my grandmother
this ex-flapper draggin me to the mall
cause she went through my stuff
and decided i didnt have enough draws

bussit boom
fruit-a-looms

grandma be crazy cruisin
you be behind her
wunderin   *what the fuck is she doin?*

                        in the fast lane
                        tailgatin time
                        trying to make the conversation last

known her all my life
still hard to break the ice

be talkin to her all loud
little red riding hood riding shotgun
suspicious of the wolf
hey grandma! what mighty big eyes for you ta have!

been drivin these streets for years
now she pretends like she cant see
nose pressed against the windshield
asking directions eyes peeled for some attention

turn signal on for the past five intersections
then she abruptly cuts you off
and wheels that brown buick skylark into the wrong parking lot
her plastic bracelets
click clack
clank 'n clinkin
down crinkly charles chestnutt
high hinkdy yellow forearm flab
wiggling through an illegal u-turn into oncoming traffic

hey grandma!

the fact that i need some clothes
to her is the most important thing in the world
unjam my nineteen year old knees from the glove compartment

squeeze out the front seat
on my way to what god willing will be my last back-to-
school sale

"youll like nordstroms they have a good selection"
walkin to the mens section
department store erection
from thinkin about past sins
me my friends and the young miss mannequins

"boy you get everything you need"   ok grandma

pickin through the bargain bin
tryin to find something she thinks is nice
something thats not too expensive
and i could bear to wear at least twice

she dont play the radio
on our sunday drives
our once-a-year september shopping spree
afraid that i'll get mad
and throw a tantrum
now that im kind of curious about what she listens to
she dont play the radio

i miss the
long distance staticky baritone shortwave gospel
gibberish
outta nashville

the Peaceway Temple's founder and overseer Prophet
   Omega
and now todays program

   Friends seen 'n unseen
   people dat are ridin' 'long in their automobeels
   peeppll that are sittin' at the table
   i greet you with the holy word peace
   fo' with my intimate mind i think constructively
   fo' yo' minds are my min' and my min' is yo' min
   and imuh sendin' out my christ mind to you you 'n you

now grandma just hum
change lanes for no reason
askin me when im going to church
i slurp the last of my vanilla shake
watching the stop lights go by

i dont know grandma im just tryin to get over
getting over usta mean your soul crossing into heaven
   not getting over the hump
      or getting over on some punk

      i just cant get into
         munchin dry fish and bread
            free lunch sandwiches on the beach with jesus

               and if he had really turned water into wine
                  my whole neighborhood be on line

now every year a bit before christmas
i see jesus reincarnated in the theater district
showin off his double dealin three card monte
mr magician parlor tricks
whistlin *how i got over*

                                    fleecin the meek
                                    spittin and playin the unhip for vics
                                    one eye out for the police
                   here come one now
                   shepherd of sheep
                   blowin a plastic shofar

"ease up cuz"
the game disappears
the playing table
flops into cardboard box litter
the apostle shills and stick men hit it
mesh into the crowd
walkin a little quicker step than everyone else
get outta dodge the pedestrians pep
                         meet you at the spot   go for self   yep   bet

tony toi's sister nica's boyfriend
showed me the tricks
in a challenge of wits
street savvy vs. booksmarts

right at the start
he bent the corner of the red card

i thought to myself thats it
another stupid ghetto nigga done slipped

los angeles summer vacation misdirection
your eyes stuck on the disfigured suicide king of hearts
the quickness in his wrists   the spiel   the con mans diss

you a straight A nigga
blam goddamn dumb ass motherfucker
this one and that is black
the red and you get paid
pick the correct shit

threw a dollar on the coach
and my dog-eared sure fired winner
was the nine of spades listenin to pot call the kettle
names

lets go again run it back black
academically enriched   pitchin a fit
but now who's gettin over?   who's schoolin who?

pardon me   who is gettin over on whom

my english teacher says never use the word get

but only other synonym comes to mind is take
what about receive?
i dont never get nothing that way

if i dont take it i wont get it
well dont use get in your writing understand?   yeah
  i get you

get busy
get back
get taken   *get* took off   i *got* mines you *get* yours

punks get got in the age of hiphop
the trained eye
can spot the *spots*
i spy . . . some proper talkin american polka dots

houseparty party-mix misfits
wallflower wild irish red-light roses
tryin to be different

slow dancin with after-images of a kind   of nigga
  that doesnt exist

reluctant hominy grit homonyms
watchin the sweat on the windows drip
come monday they
refuse to strip in gym
prefer to play tetherball
four square and hopscotch
on rainy days they play charades with race
—sounds like—
a high school fake monty python british accent
where you from old chap, london?   naw watts

say boy   that biology book explain why
            on these latin american *novelas*
            all the men got black hair and shades
            and all the women are blond love slaves
mendel dont explain that

        or if poverty is hereditary
        grandma brush some dust from the tv screen
        with the flat of her hand

i ask her how come she and ms. rudolph didnt do
  windows
she said "cause people can see you doin
  windows"

you watchin this grandma
"no" (if i ask she aint watchin)
turn the channel   mick jagger singin satisfaction
whos that   rolling stones   as in the papa was   naw as
  in gathering no moss
let me tell you bout satisfaction
in 1938 after years of hearing the white paddies
chant *nigger nigger never die, black face shiny eyed*

          my father and his partner
          came home from the second louis / schmeling
            fight
          wonderment and pride
          laid his hat down

did that male side to side jimmy stewart thing
to loosen his tie

sayin joe louis hit that man so hard
schmeling landed on the ropes
and started screaming aaaaahhhh

screamed till his corner men
came and hugged him

he say thats satisfaction
he say thats the only time he ever heard a white man
scream for real

sometimes at night
i can hear pushcart sam
the ghetto town crier
yellin at shadows
the black behind drawn curtains
it's three o clock and everything is fucked up

his left rear shopping cart wheel
wiggles wobbles and squeaks but gets no
grease
every few feet it locks and drags
leaving skid marks on the linoleum sidewalks
the earth is an open mall and this city aint nothing but
aisle 4
attention all k-mart shoppers

on sundays sam sits on a faded fallen vacant lot
refrigerator
sifting through food coupons
looking for 25 cent off pork 'n beans
playin with a tarnished brass mouthpiece
that seems to fit in the louis armstrong crease in
his lips

sam stands and works his fingers
over the plungers of an air-trumpet
tattered pin striped suit
yankee baseball hat as mute

a recycled miles davis anadizin the ghetto in silent
aluminum blue tunes?
or gabriel in pork pie hat

just like a nigga angel runnin late for work
blowin his horn after the rapture is over

every once in a while
i see the winged spirits of niggas past raise out the
rubble
doppel gangbangin ghosts of john henry
urban zeitgeist who fought and died lost and
exhausted
from diggin tunnels of love
smith and wesson hammerin against the steam
engined deus ex machina

thru stone mountains and neo-conservative
  molehills

folkloric heart attacks   bustin caps
eulogize and romanticize the guys on their way to the
  eternal haps

bumper to bumper
dead blacks

there go my brother helpin to direct the traffic
tellin fools back the fuck up   step off   step to this
                                          step to that

he helped raise me
but grandma couldnt hold him
not much can
and there he stands   no paddle in the sidecreek to the
  main stream

babblin and braggin how his is the last face lotsa
  niggas've seen

as he runs down a who's who in the neighborhood
  yearbook

see that kid over there who passed
by and waved a shy little hi
thats eric thompson

rahway class of '89
rifle club   varsity B and E team
sergeant at arms for the society of double muslims
ambition—*"I want to fuck the world, put my dick in the earth."*

for what its worth
nigga owe me fifteen hundred dollars

wuddup mutherfuckah?
when the clock rings
it rings hard

my brother has left niggas in backyards
has left niggas under some dirt

i suppose if i called up my brother said murder that nigguh
drag him to his front door

buss it boom
he do it

sometimes you have to put a mutherfucker in check
mutherfucker do wrong

you make your opening move
walk past a fool nonchalant   pull his card   take his pawn *en passant*

pin the kid in
with palms on the wall boris spassky grandmaster
   flash attack strategy

was that you who was fucken wid my cousin?

if he castles with denial

naw that wasnt me

   then you go straight to the end game
   fuck with his brain
   move his loved ones to Qe8

dont you live on straight street apt 4G
digits is 555-2468 who do we appreciate
and aint that your pop
be playin the numbers at the spot near the cab stand
wear a green fedora   tilted to the left side monday
   thru saturday
to the right sunday
thought so
            checkmate

forever playin the mindgame

the other day in psychology
while they was talkin about the oedipus and electra
   complexes

i was skimmin ahead
looking at the pictures

figurin that since i was from a broken
home
these psychosexual stages didnt apply to
me
i wasnt obsessed with no feces

though i might be orally fixated
i sucked my thumb to slumber up until my
fourteenth summer
wonder how im gonna grow up
both your parents on drugs
realistic dreamscape not much food on my
plate

house is a shooting gallery

on page 98
i came across this skinny scrawny wirebrush bristle
haired little monkey
clinging to its bogus man made surrogate mother
big red taillight eyes
a wire torso and pacifiers for breasts

no warmth no affection

i know some mothers like that

my parents were like african voodoo dolls
that their own suicidal spirits stuck syringes in

poison darts
and hat pins dipped in
liquid coping mechanisms

i used to play connect the dots with the pock marks
and scars
on my daddys arms

niggas useta tell jokes about my mother
i just lose it

nigga, your mother so stupid
when she gets on the elevator and wants to go
to the fourth floor
she press two twice

i just start cryin
dry my eyes
steady lyin bout my pops
whats my father do? oh he's in europe shootin hoops
time for young mens group

those long winded nationalistic filibusters on culture
cryptic muslim brothers the acidic citrus fruit of
islam
blacker than johnny cash in gloves and a ski mask

and tellin us how we should live our lives

. . . and you fellas should be looking for a wife
that is 7 years your junior
half past a monkeys ass and a quarter to his
balls . . .

rocky watch me pull a rabbit outta my hat
pressin up my sleeves presto!

no no anything but that
not the syllaballistic linguistic bullwinkle bullshit
please no

b lack bullack be lack beee lack ing   be
lacking

WHAT?

negro neee grooo   neeee   grooooo
neg a tive growth

if this nigga says diaspora forget it we in here for two
more hours
well then lets diaspora the fuck outta this mother-
fuckuh

no notes in my notebook
an at lunchtime me and the homies cook

huddled in the school yard
boys since the swing set
hunched over a tapedeck
rollin our shoulders keepin time with life
and catchin spiritual rec

got a puerto rican coolout
name of billy matos
spend most our time eating french fried
potatoes
when we leave its hasta luego
im hot
como un fuego

oye que pasa
heard about the tabula rasa
but im chalkboard with no chalk
soz i spends my time with the oral jabberwock
tweedledum and tweedledee
there go lewis carroll showin alice his wee wee
"The vorpal blade went snicker-snack!"

fuckin public pool pedophiliac
the big blue meanie starin at
pre-teens in bikinis

"Beware the jabberwock my son!
The jaws that bite, the claws that catch!"

Who dat? who dat? Who dat say who dat, when i say
who dat?

can you show me where he touched you

pssst check my portfolio
like jonas salk
i got the cure for
pimp limpin gangster polio
a vaccine that takes niggas off gods shit list
answers the prayers of wounded hustlers in wheel chairs
wearin 100 dollar sneakers that never touch the sidewalk

i'll grant you three wishes if you rub my lantern
oooh a little to the right
wish i may wish i might first star i see tonight

schmiel schmallzle
fizzle fazzle
still a little kid cause i like to eat razzles
flim flam-a-diddle
no time to quibble
ready set hut take the snap
and run straight up the middle

i aint in it to win it
im just trying to hook up with a crew
be on the periphery
be a back up rapper
an SIW or some shit

be response to they call
a supreme behind diana ross
a pip behind gladys knight
kokomo to joe schmoe

blaa blaa HEY!

yakkity yak gats bats n hats HOO!

put on my gear and act goofy in the video

not translucent not see through not bulletproof
kind of obtuse

opaque

a jittery kid in the national spelling bee
reluctantly leaves a metal chair
cardboard sign dangling and banging on birdlike pre-
pubescent chest
tender nipples
opaque

may i have a definition?
vague dark 'n dull hard to understand
obscure

may i have the origin?
middle english

that figures what *nothing may i have an alternate pronunciation?*

oh pah queue

can you use the word in a sentence?

when asked to put a check in the box marked race
the respondent chose opaque (non-hispanic)

opaque O-P-A-Q-U-E opaque

wearin the subway bus
public transportation deadpan ghetto face
the educated sympathetic liberal doesnt understand
i want to be ralph ellisons invisible man
peek-a-boo i see you
run the jewels

thats what i like about black people they fuck with the rules

we usta play marco polo
when the kid who couldnt swim was it . . .
ok you guys tell me if im going towards the deep end of the pool

marco! *polo!* marco! *polo!* marco blubblub-blubblub

5 10 15 20 25 30 *my cheri amour pretty little girl that i adore* 95 100
ready or not here i come

buster be in the middle of the street
yellin alli alli outs in free
and when you came out he beat you for
beatin him

when buster was it
we hid in obvious places
behind fire hydrants
under the sky
tap tap on your black ass
hidin behind the crab grass

twenty horses in a stable one got out

now we hide in the library
it be few of us in there
sittin in front of the big metal fan
squeezed in little wooden chairs
it so quiet
no hoodlums
just the mutter of bookworm bums

come february i like watching
the little kids and their parents
excited with annual pride
rush ms. biot

can i help you

you the librarian? i wanna do something on black
  history
lemme have a book on black history

what part of black history are you interested in

just black history
gimme the goddamn black history book
ms. biot be cursin waitin on march 1st
you stupid niggas get the fuck outta here

word
word is weak
shhhh quiet down
naw man a messerschmitt take out a P-38 lightning
  fighter/bomber
you crazy turn the page

the library is our barbershop
we sit around in cutoffs and dirty socks
tellin stories
who got shot
taking odds on who gonna get popped

tell the one about your sister and the jewelry shop

the one when boyfriends amos 'n andy malapropped
through life making secret get rich quick schemes

simonize your watches

american dreamers

call in mid scalp grease
hot comb
as the world turns
half dressed

the dream needs a vet
and you better be ready when it gets here

or else it pulls you into the car
by braids barrettes and screams
drive twice around the block
speakin old movie criminalese
anna go in there and case the joint
lefty knuckles and mugs
when push comes to shove
what you wont do, do for love

you would think a store in the middle of the valley
fifty yards from a freeway on ramp
would be suspicious

if a scared pajama clad light fuzzy blue house shoe
wearing ashy legged dried up
tears chubby cheeked black woman pippy long-
stocking pickaninny braids on one side
the other newly fried untied and electrified came ten
feet into the store stared

directly at the jewelry case turned slowly around
counting out loud the number of
security and sales personnel the steps to the door

sledge hammers broken glass and laughs

she wouldnt take her cut

back at the palace with a torn screen door
the american dreams mama and her sister
sit on the sofa throne
sartres' harpies reclined in repose
in the kingdom of flies lay-away and
payments
counting the take

child you better take some
shoot you earned it
take a chain or somethin
can you turn up the stereo

ms. biot sees that we've stopped reading
readies to leave
she gives us whatever books we wuz looking at

these are due in two weeks
did i tell you that im psychic
paul ronald jamal you all gonna be
lawyers doctors

whatever it is you want
apart from playin ball

another mindgame but we bite
you aint psychic

think of a number between 1 and 9 you got it?
now multiply that number by nine you got it?
now if its double digits add them up
subtract five from the total

now take that number and replace it with the corresponding letter of the alphabet

if its 1 thats an A, if its 2 thats a B, and so on
now think of a country that begins with your letter
now take the second letter of that country and think of an animal
that starts with that letter
now think of the color of that animal

you thinkin of a gray elephant right
how she know
naw fool i had a black emu
i had a brown elk

grandma
i dont want to die
like some poached animal in the serengeti
a bushman in the kalahari

tuned into radio free europe
listenin to the Prophet Omega

The Shipp Moving Co. who is located on Old Lexington city highway. They been in bidness since 19 and 54 and they specialize in movin fahn furniture, yo' furniture which is fine furniture . . . now fo' a courtesy move uh quick move or a right now move then call Shipp Movin' got menz ovah dere who are very courtesy an unner-standin' and don't mind tryin' to satisfy you the custo-ment. The company give you an estimation they don't charge you extra fo' dat and if the company move you they don't charge you any extra for a heavy piece, uh heavier piece and they got some beautiful girls ovah dere doin' the packin' 'n unpackin' now this cost you extra. But what is a little extra for safety ssss? Yo' glasses don't be broken. Yo' silverware wrapped nice . . . the very things in which you treasure wrapped and unwrapped took down and put up. Now that's the Shipp Movin' Co., you may call them at 242-5381 thats 242-5381, 242-5381

think i'll go to school
get me some of that United Negro College Fund money
  lou rawls
and that marathon parade of fading hollywood stars
raise every holiday

fool, what you gonna take up in college?
space

But I sighted a distant horizon

Where the sky line encircled the sea

And I throbbed with a burning desire

To travel this immensity.

JAMAICA

KINCAID

FROM

Annie John

"Gwen"

ON OPENING DAY, I walked to my new school alone. It was the first and last time that such a thing would happen. All around me were other people my age—twelve years—girls and boys, dressed in their school uniforms, marching off to school. They all seemed to know each other, and as they met they would burst into laughter, slapping each other on the shoulder and back, telling each other things that must have made for much happiness. I saw some girls wearing the same uniform as my own, and my heart just longed for them to say something to me, but the most they could do to include me was to smile and nod in my direction as they walked on arm in arm. I could hardly blame them for not paying more attention to me. Everything about me was so new: my uniform was new, my shoes were new, my hat was new, my shoulder ached from the weight of my new books in my new bag; even the road I walked on was new, and I must have put my feet down as if I weren't sure the ground was solid. At school, the yard was filled with more of these girls and their most sure-of-themselves gaits. When I looked at them, they made up a sea. They were walking in and out among the beds of flowers, all across the fields, all across the courtyard, in and out of classrooms. Except for me, no one seemed a stranger to anything or anyone. Hearing the way they greeted each other, I couldn't be sure that they hadn't all come out of the same woman's belly, and at the same time, too. Looking at them, I was suddenly glad that because I had wanted to avoid an argument with my mother I had eaten all my breakfast, for now I surely would have fainted if I had been in any more weakened a condition.

I knew where my classroom was, because my mother and I had kept an appointment at the school a week before. There I met some of my teachers and was shown the ins and outs of everything. When I saw it then, it was nice and orderly and empty and smelled just scrubbed. Now it smelled of girls milling around, fresh ink in inkwells, new books, chalk and erasers. The girls in my classroom acted even more familiar with each other. I was sure I would never be able to tell them apart just from looking at them, and I was sure that I would never be able to tell them apart from the sound of their voices.

When the school bell rang at half past eight, we formed ourselves into the required pairs and filed into the auditorium for morning prayers and hymn-singing. Our headmistress gave us a little talk, welcoming the new students and welcoming back the old students, saying that she hoped we had all left our bad ways behind us, that we would be good examples for each other and bring greater credit to our school than any of the other groups of girls who had been there before us. My palms were wet, and quite a few times the ground felt as if it were seesawing under my feet, but that didn't stop me from taking in a few things. For instance, the headmistress, Miss Moore. I knew right away that she had come to Antigua from England, for she looked like a prune left out of its jar a long time and she sounded as if she had borrowed her voice from an owl. The way she said, "Now, girls . . ." When she was just standing still there, and listening to some of the other activities, her gray eyes going all around the room hoping to see something wrong, her throat would beat up and down as if a fish fresh out of water were caught inside. I wondered if she even smelled like a fish. Once when I didn't wash, my mother had given me a long scolding about it, and she ended by saying that it was the only thing she didn't like about English people: they didn't wash often enough, or wash properly when they finally did. My mother had said, "Have you ever noticed how they smell as if they had been bottled up in a fish?" On either side of Miss Moore stood our other teachers, women and men—mostly women. I recognized Miss George, our music teacher;

Miss Nelson, our homeroom teacher; Miss Edward, our history and geography teacher; and Miss Newgate, our algebra and geometry teacher. I had met them the day my mother and I were at school. I did not know who the others were, and I did not worry about it. Since they were teachers, I was sure it wouldn't be long before, because of some misunderstanding, they would be thorns in my side.

We walked back to our classroom the same way we had come, quite orderly and, except for a few whispered exchanges, quite silent. But no sooner were we back in our classroom than the girls were in each other's laps, arms wrapped around necks. After peeping over my shoulder left and right, I sat down in my seat and wondered what would become of me. There were twenty of us in my class, and we were seated at desks arranged five in a row, four rows deep. I was at a desk in the third row, and this made me even more miserable. I hated to be seated so far away from the teacher, because I was sure I would miss something she said. But, even worse, if I was out of my teacher's sight all the time, how could she see my industriousness and quickness at learning things? And, besides, only dunces were seated so far to the rear, and I could not bear to be thought a dunce. I was now staring at the back of a shrubby-haired girl seated in the front row—the seat I most coveted, since it was directly in front of the teacher's desk. At that moment, the girl twisted herself around, stared at me, and said, "You are Annie

John? We hear you are very bright." It was a good thing Miss Nelson walked in right then, for how would it have appeared if I had replied, "Yes, that is completely true"—the very thing that was on the tip of my tongue.

As soon as Miss Nelson walked in, we came to order and stood up stiffly at our desks. She said to us, "Good morning, class," half in a way that someone must have told her was the proper way to speak to us and half in a jocular way, as if we secretly amused her. We replied, "Good morning, Miss," in unison and in a respectful way, at the same time making a barely visible curtsy, also in unison. When she had seated herself at her desk, she said to us, "You may sit now," and we did. She opened the roll book, and as she called out our names each of us answered, "Present, Miss." As she called out our names, she kept her head bent over the book, but when she called out my name and I answered with the customary response she looked up and smiled at me and said, "Welcome, Annie." Everyone, of course, then turned and looked at me. I was sure it was because they could hear the loud racket my heart was making in my chest.

It was the first day of a new term, Miss Nelson said, so we would not be attending to any of our usual subjects; instead, we were to spend the morning in contemplation and reflection and writing something she described as an "autobiographical essay." In the afternoon, we would read aloud to each other our autobiographical essays. (I knew quite well about "autobiography" and "essay," but reflection and contemplation! A day at school spent in such a way! Of course, in most books all the good people were always contemplating and reflecting before they did anything. Perhaps in her mind's eye she could see our futures and, against all prediction, we turned out to be good people.) On hearing this, a huge sigh went up from the girls. Half the sighs were in happiness at the thought of sitting and gazing off into clear space, the other half in unhappiness at the misdeeds that would have to go unaccomplished. I joined the happy half, because I knew it would please Miss Nelson, and, my own selfish interest aside, I liked so much the way she wore her ironed hair and her long-sleeved blouse and box-pleated skirt that I wanted to please her.

The morning was uneventful enough: a girl spilled ink from her inkwell all over her uniform; a girl broke her pen nib and then made a big to-do about replacing it; girls twisted and turned in their seats and pinched each other's bottoms; girls passed notes to each other. All this Miss Nelson must have seen and heard, but she didn't say anything—only kept reading her book: an elaborately illustrated edition of *The Tempest*, as later, passing by her desk, I saw. Midway in the morning, we were told to go out and stretch our legs and breathe some fresh air for a few minutes; when we returned, we were given glasses of cold lemonade and a slice of bun to refresh us.

As soon as the sun stood in the middle of the sky, we

were sent home for lunch. The earth may have grown an inch or two larger between the time I had walked to school that morning and the time I went home to lunch, for some girls made a small space for me in their little band. But I couldn't pay much attention to them; my mind was on my new surroundings, my new teacher, what I had written in my nice new notebook with its black-all-mixed-up-with-white cover and smooth lined pages (so glad was I to get rid of my old notebooks, which had on their covers a picture of a wrinkled-up woman wearing a crown on her head and a neckful and armfuls of diamonds and pearls—their pages so coarse, as if they were made of cornmeal). I flew home. I must have eaten my food. I flew back to school. By half past one, we were sitting under a flamboyant tree in a secluded part of our schoolyard, our autobiographical essays in hand. We were about to read aloud what we had written during our morning of contemplation and reflection.

In response to Miss Nelson, each girl stood up and read her composition. One girl told of a much revered and loved aunt who now lived in England and of how much she looked forward to one day moving to England to live with her aunt; one girl told of her brother studying medicine in Canada and the life she imagined he lived there (it seemed quite odd to me); one girl told of the fright she had when she dreamed she was dead, and of the matching fright she had when she woke and found that she wasn't (everyone laughed at this, and Miss Nelson had to call us to order over and over); one girl told of how her oldest sister's best friend's cousin's best friend (it was a real rigmarole) had gone on a Girl Guide jamboree held in Trinidad and met someone who millions of years ago had taken tea with Lady Baden-Powell; one girl told of an excursion she and her father had made to Redonda, and of how they had seen some booby birds tending their chicks. Things went on in that way, all so playful, all so imaginative. I began to wonder about what I had written, for it was the opposite of playful and it was the opposite of imaginative. What I had written was heartfelt, and, except for the very end, it was all too true. The afternoon was wearing itself thin. Would my turn ever come? What should I do, finding myself in a world of new girls, a world in which I was not even near the center?

It was a while before I realized that Miss Nelson was calling on me. My turn at last to read what I had written. I got up and started to read, my voice shaky at first, but since the sound of my own voice had always been a calming potion to me, it wasn't long before I was reading in such a way that, except for the chirp of some birds, the hum of bees looking for flowers, the silvery rush-rush of the wind in the trees, the only sound to be heard was my voice as it rose and fell in sentence after sentence. At the end of my reading, I thought I was imagining the upturned faces on which were looks of adoration, but I was not; I thought I was imagining, too, some eyes brimming over with tears, but again I was not. Miss Nelson said that she would like to borrow what I had written to read for herself, and that it would be placed on the shelf with the books that made up our own class library, so that it would be available to any girl who wanted to read it. This is what I had written:

"When I was a small child, my mother and I used to go down to Rat Island on Sundays right after church, so that I could bathe in the sea. It was at a time when I was thought to have weak kidneys and a bath in the sea had been recommended as a strengthening remedy. Rat Island wasn't a place many people went to anyway, but by climbing down some rocks my mother had found a place that nobody seemed to have ever been. Since this bathing in the sea was a medicine and not a picnic, we had to bathe without wearing swimming costumes. My mother was a superior swimmer. When she plunged into the seawater, it was as if she had always lived there. She would go far out if it was safe to do so, and she could tell just by looking at the way the waves beat if it was safe to do so. She could tell if a shark was nearby, and she had never been stung by a jellyfish. I, on the other hand, could not swim at all. In fact, if I was in water up to my knees I was sure that I was drowning. My mother had tried everything to get me swimming, from using a coaxing method to just throwing me without a word into the water. Nothing worked. The only way I could go into the water was if I was on my mother's back, my arms clasped tightly around her neck, and she would then swim around not too far from the shore. It was only then that I could forget how big the sea was, how far down the bottom could be, and how filled up it was with things that couldn't understand a nice hallo. When we swam around in this way, I would think how much we were like the pictures of sea mammals I had seen, my mother and I, naked in the seawater, my mother sometimes singing to me a song in a French patois I did not yet understand, or sometimes not saying anything at all. I would place my ear against her neck, and it was as if I were listening to a giant shell, for all the sounds around me—the sea, the wind, the birds screeching—would seem as if they came from inside her, the way the sounds of the sea are in a seashell. Afterward, my mother would take me back to the shore, and I would lie there just beyond the farthest reach of a big wave and watch my mother as she swam and dove.

"One day, in the midst of watching my mother swim and dive, I heard a commotion far out at sea. It was three ships going by, and they were filled with people. They must have been celebrating something, for the ships would blow their horns and the people would cheer in response. After they passed out of view, I turned back to look at my mother, but I could not see her. My eyes searched the small area of water where she should have been, but I couldn't find her. I stood up and started to call out her name, but no sound would come out of my throat. A huge black space then opened up in front of me and I fell inside it. I couldn't see what was in front of me and I couldn't hear anything around me. I couldn't think of anything except that my mother was no longer near me. Things went on in this way for I don't know how long. I don't know what, but something drew my eye in one direction. A little bit out of the area in which she usually swam was my mother, just sitting and tracing patterns on a large rock. She wasn't paying any attention to me, for she didn't know that I had missed her. I was glad to see her and started jumping up and down and waving to her. Still she didn't see me, and then I started to cry, for it dawned on me that, with all that water between us and I being unable to swim, my mother could stay there forever and the only way I would be able to wrap my arms around her again was if it pleased her or if I took a boat. I cried until I wore myself out. My tears ran down into my mouth, and it was the first time that I realized tears had a bitter and salty taste. Finally, my mother came ashore. She was, of course, alarmed when she saw my face, for I had let the tears just dry there and they left a stain. When I told her what had happened, she hugged me so close that it was hard to breathe, and she told me that nothing could be farther from the truth—that she would never ever leave me. And though she said it over and over again, and though I felt better, I could not wipe out of my mind the feeling I had had when I couldn't find her.

"The summer just past, I kept having a dream about my mother sitting on the rock. Over and over I would have the dream—only in it my mother never came back, and sometimes my father would join her. When he joined her, they would both sit tracing patterns on the rock, and it must have been amusing, for they would always make each other laugh. At first, I didn't say anything, but when I began to have the dream again and again, I finally told my mother. My mother became instantly distressed; tears came to her eyes, and, taking me in her arms, she told me all the same things she had told me on the day at the sea, and this time the memory of the dark time when I felt I would never see her again did not come back to haunt me."

I didn't exactly tell a lie about the last part. That is just what would have happened in the old days. But actually the past year saw me launched into young-ladyness, and when I told my mother of my dream—my nightmare, really—I was greeted with a turned back and a warning against eating certain kinds of fruit in an unripe state just before going to bed. I placed the old days' version before my classmates because, I thought, I couldn't bear to show my mother in a bad light before people who hardly knew her. But the real truth was that I couldn't bear to have anyone see how deep in disfavor I was with my mother.

As we walked back to the classroom, I in the air, my classmates on the ground, jostling each other to say some words of appreciation and congratulation to me, my head felt funny, as if it had swelled up to the size of, and weighed no more than, a blown-up balloon. Often I had been told by my mother not to feel proud of anything I had done and in the next breath that I couldn't feel enough pride about something I had done. Now I tossed from one to the other: my head bowed down to the ground, my head high up in the air. I looked at these girls surrounding me, my heart filled with just-sprung-up love, and I wished then and there to spend the rest of my life only with them.

As we approached our classroom, I felt a pinch on my arm. It was an affectionate pinch, I could tell. It was the girl who had earlier that day asked me if my name was Annie John. Now she told me that her name was Gweneth Joseph, and reaching into the pocket of her tunic, she brought out a small rock and presented it to me. She had found it, she said, at the foot of a sleeping volcano. The rock was black, and it felt rough in my hands, as if it had been through a lot. I immediately put it to my nose to see what it smelled like. It smelled of lavender, because Gweneth Joseph had kept it wrapped in a handkerchief doused in that scent. It may have been in that moment that we fell in love. Later, we could never agree on when it was. That afternoon, we walked home together, she going a little out of her usual way, and we exchanged likes and dislikes, our jaws dropping and eyes widening when we saw how similar they were. We separated ourselves from the other girls, and they, understanding everything, left us alone. We cut through a tamarind grove, we cut through a cherry-tree grove, we passed down the lane where all the houses had elaborate hedges growing in front, so that nothing was visible but the upstairs windows. When we came to my street, parting was all but unbearable. "Tomorrow," we said, to cheer each other up.

Gwen and I were soon inseparable. If you saw one, you saw the other. For me, each day began as I waited for Gwen to come by and fetch me for school. My heart beat fast as I stood in the front yard of our house waiting to see Gwen as she rounded the bend in our street. The sun, already way up in the sky so early in the morning, shone on her, and the whole street became suddenly empty so that Gwen and everything about her were perfect, as if she were in a picture. Her panama hat, with the navy blue and gold satin ribbon—our school colors—around the brim, sat lopsided on her head, for her head was small and she never seemed to get the correct-size hat, and it had to be anchored with a piece of elastic running under her chin. The pleats in the tunic of her uniform were in place, as was to be expected. Her cotton socks fit neatly around her ankles, and her shoes shone from just being polished. If a small breeze blew, it would ruffle the ribbons in her short, shrubby hair and the hem of her tunic; if the hem of her tunic was disturbed in that way, I would then be able to see her knees. She had bony knees and they were always ash-colored, as if she had just finished giving them a good scratch or had just finished saying her prayers. The breeze might also blow back the brim of her hat, and since she always walked with her head held down I might then be able to see her face: a small, flattish nose; lips the shape of a saucer broken evenly in two; wide, high cheekbones; ears pinned back close against her head—which was always set in a serious way, as if she were going over in her mind some of the many things we had hit upon that were truly a mystery to us. (Though once I told her that about her face, and she said that really she had only been thinking about me. I didn't look to make sure, but I felt as if my whole skin had become covered with millions of tiny red boils and that shortly I would explode with happiness.) When finally she reached me, she would look up and we would both smile and say softly, "Hi." We'd set off for school side by side, our feet in step, not touching but feeling as if we were joined at the shoulder, hip, and ankle, not to mention heart.

As we walked together, we told each other things we had judged most private and secret: things we had overheard our parents say, dreams we had had the night before, the things we were really afraid of; but especially we told of our love for each other. Except for the ordinary things that naturally came up, I never told her about my changed feeling for my mother. I could see in what high regard Gwen held me, and I couldn't bear for her to see the great thing I had had once and then lost without an explanation. By the time we got to school, our chums often seemed overbearing, with their little comments on the well-pressedness of each other's uniforms, or on the neatness of their schoolbooks, or on how much they approved of the way Miss Nelson was wearing her hair these days. A few other girls were having much the same experience as Gwen and I, and when we heard comments of this kind we would look at each other and roll up our eyes and toss our hands in the air—a way of saying how above such concerns we were. The gesture was an exact copy, of course, of what we had seen our mothers do.

My life in school became just the opposite of my first morning. I went from being ignored, with hardly a glance from anyone, to having girls vie for my friendship, or at least for more than just a passing acquaintanceship. Both my classmates and my teachers noticed how quick I was at learning things. I was soon given responsibility for overseeing the class in the teacher's absence. At first, I was a little taken aback by this, but then I got used to it. I indulged many things, especially if they would end in a laugh or something touching. I would never dillydally with a decision, always making up my mind right away about the thing in front of me. Sometimes, seeing my old frail self in a girl, I would defend her; sometimes, seeing my old frail self in a girl, I would be heartless and cruel. It all went over quite well, and I became very popular.

My so recently much-hated body was now a plus: I excelled at games and was named captain of a volleyball team. As I was favored by my classmates inside and outside the classroom, so was I favored by my teachers—though only inside the classroom, for I had become notorious to them for doing forbidden things. If sometimes I stood away from myself and took a look at who I had become, I couldn't be more surprised at what I saw. But since who I had become earned me the love and devotion of Gwen and the other girls, I was only egged on to find new and better ways to entertain them. I don't know what invisible standard was set, or by whom or exactly when, but eight of us met it, and soon to the other girls we were something to comment on favorably or unfavorably, as the case might be.

It was in a nook of some old tombstones—a place discovered by girls going to our school long before we were born—shaded by trees with trunks so thick it would take four arm's lengths to encircle them, that we would sit and talk about the things we said were on our minds that day. On our minds every day were our breasts and their refusal to budge out of our chests. On hearing somewhere that if a boy rubbed your breasts they would quickly swell up, I passed along this news. Since in the world we occupied and hoped forever to occupy boys were banished, we had to make do with ourselves. What perfection we found in each other, sitting on these tombstones of long-dead people who had been the masters of our ancestors! Nothing in particular really troubled us except for the annoyance of a fly colliding with our lips, sticky from eating fruits; a bee wanting to nestle in our hair; the breeze suddenly blowing too strong. We were sure that the much-talked-about future that everybody was preparing us for would never come, for we had such a powerful feeling against it, and why shouldn't our will prevail this time? Sometimes when we looked at each other, it was all we could do not to cry out with happiness.

My own special happiness was, of course, with Gwen. She would stand in front of me trying to see into my murky black eyes—a way, she said, to tell exactly what I was thinking. After a short while, she would give up, saying, "I can't make out a thing—only my same old face." I would then laugh at her and kiss her on the neck, sending her into a fit of shivers, as if someone had exposed her to a cold draft when she had a fever. Sometimes when she spoke to me, so overcome with feeling would I be that I was no longer able to hear what she said, I could only make out her mouth as it moved up and down. I told her that I wished I had been named Enid, after Enid Blyton, the author of the first books I had discovered on my own and liked. I told her that when I was younger I had been afraid of my mother's dying, but that since I had met Gwen this didn't matter so much. Whenever I spoke of my mother to her, I was always sure to turn the corners of my mouth down, to show my scorn. I said that I could not wait for us to grow up so that we could live in a house of our own. I had already picked out the house. It was a gray one, with many rooms, and it was in the lane where all the houses had high, well-trimmed hedges. With all my plans she agreed, and I am sure that if she had had any plans of her own I would have agreed with them also.

NTOZAKE

SHANGE

FROM

Betsey Brown

BETSEY COULD HARDLY WAIT to tell Veejay and Charlotte Ann what had happened at her house. She wanted to brag that she herself had run old Bernice out the house. When she saw Charlotte Ann talking through the fence to Seymour Bournes, who was from the high school and a friend of Eugene Boyd, she rushed up. Charlotte Ann's eyes were sparkling and her hips were wiggling totally out of control.

"Charlotte Ann, how are you doing? Hi, Seymour," Betsey blurted, full of herself and inquisitive bout the relationship tween Seymour and Charlotte Ann, who'd always said she was ascared of boys, but apparently not this one. Seymour was a tallish boy with curly black hair and large ears that flew from the sides of his head like propellers. They would have looked like ordinary ears had his face been any fuller, but Seymour's face was thin, like a taffy pulled way far out. Seymour had seen Betsey before, but didn't actually know her. Her cousin Charlie played ball real good, but it was Eugene who'd pointed her out to him. Eugene liked her. As a matter of fact, Eugene had taken to being friends with Charlie just so he'd have a reason to visit, but Betsey and Charlotte Ann knew nothing of this. All Charlotte Ann knew was Betsey was beside herself about something that would have to wait till Seymour went cross the street to class.

Betsey saw Veejay coming through the schoolyard with her books up under her left arm, as always chewing gum to make sounds like a popping snare drum. Realizing that Charlotte Ann and Seymour were no longer aware of her, Betsey ran toward Veejay yelling, "Hey, Veejay, guess what?"

"What ya mean, 'guess what'? Can't you say hello or good day or something?" Veejay retorted tween smacks of cherry gum.

"Well, Good Day, then, Miz Veejay, M'am." The two girls laughed and kept on tittering M'ams and Good Mornings till Betsey told Veejay bout Bernice and how bad they'd all been and how Bernice had gotten her walking papers and the house was theirs again. Betsey'd opened her lunch bag awready, chewing on a bright apple, waiting for Veejay to cry out with a "Go on, girl" or "I bet that was a lot of fun," but Veejay was just looking mad and hurt all at once.

"Whatsa matter, Veejay? She's gone now. That's what counts, isn't it? She told on us. She would have ruined everything."

"Betsey, you know what my mama does for a living?"

"No."

"Well, she takes care of nasty white chirren who act up like y'all acted up this morning. She don't do it cause she likes it neither. She does it so I could have clothes and food and a place to live. That's all that Bernice woman was trying to do, and you so stupid you don't even know if she's got somewhere to live or if she's got chirren of her own in Arkansas. Y'all act like white people, always trying to make things hard on the colored. Lying on em and making a mess of things. Thinking it's so funny. I don't even know if I want to be your friend. That could have been my mama lost her job on accounta you and your ol' tree. You shouldn't a been up no tree no how, big as you are. You don't have no sense at all."

Veejay turned to go anywhere away from Betsey. She'd known that Betsey was from over there where the rich colored lived, but she liked her anyway. Till now, that is. Now Betsey was the same as anybody who made fun of her mother for doing daywork and looking after white children while her own waited anxiously at the door for her to come home. It was one thing to take mess from white folks, cause that was to be expected, but to have the colored—or the "Negro," as Betsey would say—do it too was hurting to Veejay, who just kept mumbling, "That coulda been my mama and you don't care."

"Veejay, I didn't mean any harm." Betsey rushed alongside Veejay, who wouldn't look at her. "Really, I didn't think, that's all. I'll tell my mother that it was all my fault. I will, Veejay, I promise. Just please stay my friend." Betsey tugged Veejay's arm, wanting her to stop so they could talk before Mrs. Mitchell quieted the class for morning announcements about Assembly, band practice, girls' volleyball, and the Pledge of Allegiance and the Lord's Prayer.

Veejay stopped. "Take your hands off me. Betsey Brown, you a selfish somebody. I don't want you to call my name. And don't you tell nobody that I'm your friend, or that I ever was, ya hear me."

Veejay stalked off to class, leaving Betsey on the stairwell with a half-eaten apple and a lot on her mind.

It was true that Veejay wore the same plaid skirt and white blouse every other day, but Betsey thought that was cause Veejay wanted it that way. Veejay'd never invited her or Charlotte Ann to visit her at home, either. And it was always Veejay who had words from her mama on what white folks were really like.

A heavy red glow came over Betsey's body. Shame. She was ashamed of herself and her sisters and Charlie and Allard. Veejay was right. Bernice just talked funny was all. Betsey'd passed over the paper bags fulla worn-out clothes, the two shoes of that woven cotton, fraying by the toes, and the calluses on the palms of the woman's hands. Betsey Brown had been so busy seeing to herself and the skies, she'd let a woman who coulda been Veejay's mama look a fool and lose her job.

Betsey threw the apple in the trash and peeked

round her carefully. She was gonna run home fast as she could, to see if she could catch her mother and tell her the truth. Maybe there was time to stop Bernice from leaving. Why, Betsey didn't know if Bernice had a girl her own age or not. Betsey didn't know if Bernice had anyplace to go, or anyone to go to. Betsey had to get home and apologize to Bernice.

It was awfully hard to sneak out of Clark School once you were in it. Hall patrols and Mr. Wichiten wandered arbitrarily hither and yon, but Betsey made a good run for it, down the south corridor to the door that opened toward the high school. Sometimes that door was locked or chained to keep out vagrants or bad elements, which really meant gangs, but today the door was open and out Betsey went, praying she'd catch her mother or Bernice to say "I'm sorry, please stay."

But all the running in the world and all the praying in the world couldn't catch up with the misery Bernice Calhoun knew that morning. Bernice was stepping up into the Hodiamont streetcar when Betsey spied her grandma on the front porch chattering with the wind bout what a blessing it was that trashy country gal was gone. How it was goin' to take days to put the house back in order. Betsey backed down from the porch before her grandma could lay eyes on her. Running round the back she saw her mother on her hands and knees cleaning the chicken grease off the floor. Mr. Jeff was in the parlor hanging the curtains back up.

"Betsey, what are you doing home?" Jane asked over

her shoulder. Her hands were sudsy and sweat rimmed her brow, but she didn't seem to be in a bad mood like Betsey expected.

"I came home to help clean up, Mama, and I wanted to tell you something, too."

"Don't worry, darling, I know you did your best this morning. I'm just going to have to screen these ladies more carefully from now on. Really, Betsey, I don't believe the house has ever been quite this much a mess. All because I didn't check the references, I guess. Can't be too careful nowadays."

"But, Mama, don't you want me to help? It's my fault. I didn't do what you asked me to do."

"Betsey, you go back to school where you belong. I never expected you to run this house all by yourself. That's why I hired that Calhoun woman. But you live and you learn."

"Mama, that's not what I meant."

"Doesn't matter, sweetheart." Jane rose from the floor, wiping her hands on the back of her pants she'd rolled above her knees, and went to the table to write a note. She looked like a teenager, with a scarf over her bangs and a short-sleeved cotton shirt tied at the waist. "Just get along back to school before you're marked truant, okay? Here's a note to give to Mr. Wichiten that says you've been home helping me."

"Mama, it was all my fault."

Jane drew Betsey close to her, tugging her ponytail, and said in a soft voice: "I don't want to hear any more of that, you understand? You did the best you could." With that Jane patted Betsey on the rear: "Off to school with you now. Be good."

Betsey didn't want to go back to school. Veejay'd be there, who usedta be her friend. She didn't want to go to her room either, or the basement where she'd made all the hateful plans to get rid of Bernice. She stole past her mother up the back stairs and out her window to her tree. The same tree that had started it all.

Closer to the sky and clouds, Betsey felt some of the pain wear away. She swore she'd do her best not to hurt or embarrass another Negro as long as she lived. She prayed Bernice would find another place with children not half so bad as she was. She asked God to let Veejay be her friend again. She decided not to go back to school, but to do penance instead. She sat in her tree on her knees till every bone in her body ached. Then she curled up on her favorite branch and wept for having cared so little. It could have been Veejay's mama. Maybe Veejay's mama talked funny too, but that didn't make her less a somebody, or liable to the antics of a whimsical girl who sometimes put dreams before real life, or confused them completely. It was absolutely impossible for her to have anything in common with nasty white children who bothered Veejay's mother. It was absolutely impossible for the colored to have somethin so much akin to the ways of white folks.

Seemed like her tree'd made a cradle for her and

rocked her off to sleep. Betsey was nigh on heaven's doorstep with the rustling and caws of the approaching evening, but a foreign motion interrupted her dreams. Swish. Blop. Blop. Swish. Blop. Blop. Charlie and none other than Eugene Boyd were throwing the ball over her curved body through the leaves, the limbs, the wind. Quite a challenge to Charlie's mind: make Betsey the basket and not wake her. That was the game. If his simple-minded cousin sleep in a tree at her age, she deserved whatever a body could think up. Eugene on the other hand had every intention of waking the beauty up. If he needed a basketball, so be it. Charlie took the girl for granted, maybe cause she was his cousin or maybe cause she was not his type. Eugene wasn't exactly dawdling neath the awakening Betsey, who almost lost her balance when she realized that indeed it was the very Eugene Boyd from Soldan leaping up the tree trunk to dunk the ball on the other side of her head.

"What are y'all doing? Do I look like a basketball court to you, Charlie?"

Betsey immediately thought that Charlie'd brought Eugene over just to taunt her and make her look bad. Suddenly she changed her demeanor.

"Hi, Eugene. I'm Bets . . . Elizabeth, Charlie's cousin. He stays with us here. Oh, but I guess you know that awready."

Betsey didn't know what to do. If she climbed down the tree, they'd think she was a tomboy. If she went through her window, she'd lose sight of Eugene. If she stayed where she was, they might knock her out of the tree. Not on purpose, but every shot is not a perfect one, not even for the likes of Eugene Boyd. Betsey sat up where she was, pulling her skirt over her knees to hide the scratch marks and to seem more grown, she thought. At least she wouldn't be up in a tree with her skirt hung up all round her waist like she was ten, or she didn't know that boys liked to look up girls' dresses, big boys too. She knew that cause Charlie talked a lot, but Charlie had disappeared to the back where the real basketball net was justa yearning for him.

"Come on, Gene, let's play ball." Charlie's voice floated round the edge of the house.

Eugene just kept looking at Betsey up on her perch with her hands over her knees and cheeks blushing like strawberries.

"You always stay up there?"

"No, I'm not always up here. I come up here to think is all."

Betsey didn't know what else to say. She didn't want Eugene Boyd to think she was weird. Then, on the other hand, she didn't think it was weird to stay in her tree, comforted and free as she was when boys weren't throwing balls over her head.

"What you thinkin bout up there? Your boyfriend?"

"No, oh, I always think about him when I'm alone. He's so handsome and very tall, but he's not from round here. He's from somewhere else."

"Where? Sumner? Beaumont? I wanna know cause if he's not as good looking as me, or a center forward like me, or nearby, I'd like to be considered, or rather, I'd like to come and visit with you sometime. Unless he's always on your mind."

Betsey perked up. She looked all over the tree for some advice, some indication of what to do next. What should she say? How should she move? Where were her pretty dresses? Wasn't she supposed to have on a glorious dress at a moment like this? Eugene Boyd was at the foot of her tree. This was important.

"Could you wait just one minute? I'll be right down. I'd like to talk to you a little bit longer, if you don't mind. My boyfriend lives far away from here, don't worry about him, okay?"

Betsey somehow finessed her way to the balcony, looking like a trapeze artist. Once she reached it she jumped through her window, onto her bed, about to scream with joy and surprise. Eugene. Eugene Boyd was downstairs. In minutes she'd oiled her legs, twisted her ponytail, washed her face, and put on her Sunday-school dress with the polka dots and the ribbon that tied just beneath her almost breasts. With a giant sigh and a smile right behind it, she took the front stairs very slowly, step by step, as if she were in a wedding procession. Then she forgot herself and skipped every other step, reaching the front door in a very unladylike sweat.

"Hi, here I am."

Betsey waved to Eugene, who was still over by

the side of the house looking up at her tree. The two of them were one big smile trying to cover itself up. Charlie'd left Eugene with the ball and gone off on his bike to razz the white girls, but Eugene had found his adventure right on Charlie's front porch.

"What'd you say your boyfriend's name was?"

"Oh, it doesn't matter, believe me. I watched you play the other day. You're so good." Betsey scooped up her skirt and sat on the stoop, while Eugene dribbled and bounced and dunked and turned this way and that, doing his best to impress her and get close to her. He dribbled the ball up and down the steps, asking her questions, like how old she was and did she like to dance and had she ever seen the Shirelles. Betsey was in a sweet daze through most of the conversation. She liked the talk best when Eugene dribbled the ball right next to her dress, so his leg or hand touched her shoulders. She liked the shape of his calf under his pants and the smell of his dampness mixed with the evening's.

"I guess you'll be going when Charlie comes back, huh?" Betsey looked away as she felt out Eugene's intentions.

"Why would I do that, when I came to see you? I see ol' loud-mouthed Charlie every day."

With that Eugene looped the ball round Betsey's back and caught it so his arms were on either side of her, his face directly in front of her. Betsey tried to keep her eyes open. In the movies, people closed their eyes when their faces almost touched, but that was almost kissing and Betsey'd never been kissed. She tried to keep her eyes open and Eugene kept looking in them, coming closer and closer till their lips met and Betsey's eyes closed of their own accord.

This kiss was soft and light, like petals of protea or Thai orchids. This kiss was a river wisp and innocent as dawn. It never stopped. They breathed a little and their lips parted as simply as they'd joined.

Eugene backed up and flung the ball through the air. Betsey lilted about in her glory.

"Maybe I'll come back by here, if it's awright with you? You sure are pretty, too pretty to be Charlie's cousin."

"Oh, if you were to come by, I'm sure I'll be around somewhere."

"What about your boyfriend who's so handsome?"

"Oh, I forgot about that, but don't you worry. He'll never find out. Really, he lives very far away," Betsey cooed, knowing the closest she'd ever come to having a boyfriend was this boy standing right in front of her.

"Betsey—oh, no, I'm sorry—Elizabeth, may I kiss you again? You kiss so good."

Eugene drew up next to Betsey and put his face real close to hers one more time, but Betsey's eyes didn't try to stay open. Betsey's eyes lowered and words she'd heard from Vida somehow strayed from her lips: "I think that might be a bit forward, Eugene." Then she stood glowing right next to him, so the hem of her dress danced along his back. "Maybe if you were to come calling again, I might see things differently."

Betsey was thinking now on what she'd heard Liliana

and Mavis discussing. Some "she" out there getting it or giving it to Eugene Boyd himself. No. He could wait till some other time. She needed to know if he was serious; besides, Vida had come out on the porch to crochet with the sunset and to make sure this darned boy went on his way.

"Grandma, this is Eugene Boyd. He's a friend of Charlie's."

Vida began her crocheting, some afghan for one of her daughters, swinging in the rocker reserved for her. "I suppose that's why you've got your Sunday dress on and Charlie's gone to the store. Good Evening, young man. Boyd. Seems like I've heard that name before."

"Yes, Grandma. Eugene plays ball for Soldan."

"No, that's not what I mean. I mean I think there's some Boyds from Columbia, or maybe they were from Charlotte. Carolinians, ya know."

"No, M'am. My folks are from Mississippi."

"Oh, what a shame. I thought you might be a Boyd."

Betsey and Eugene looked at each other, eyes twinkling, but fully aware they'd had their time for the day. Eugene teasingly dribbled the ball to Betsey, who took it up in rhythm. After all, she was Charlie's cousin.

"Good evening, M'am. It was nice to meet you." Eugene waved to Vida, who looked up, nodded, and went right on crocheting. Then Eugene turned to Betsey and whispered, "Maybe next time you're up in your tree, you'll be thinking on me." He pecked her on the cheek. "See ya."

Eugene began to walk on down the street, but turned round to shout, "See ya soon, Elizabeth Brown."

Betsey watched her new friend till he was completely out of sight.

"You gointa turn into a statue, if ya stay there much longer," Vida chided.

"Oh Grandma, you don't understand."

"That's what you think. Now you go on and get out of that dress before your mama wakes up and finds out you've been entertaining on the street."

"Oh Grandma, I was not. He came to see Charlie."

"Charlie's not here, Betsey. Anybody could tell you that. So if the boy came to see Charlie, why was he so busy talking to you? You don't look like Charlie. So don't call something what it's not. That little fresh boy came by here to see you."

"Grandma, that's just not true."

"That dress does more telling than your mouth'll ever do. Now, get on with ya. I mean to tell your mother to give you a good talking to. Now these boys gointa come creeping around. There's only so much a girl can do."

"Grandma, stop. Why do you have to say something to Mama. We were sitting here talking, that's all."

"That's all for now. A girl's got to think on her future."

"Think on my future? Grandma, that's such a long way off. Let's think on right now. I'm gonna change my clothes and you won't say anything to Mama, okay?"

"If ya get a move on maybe, maybe not."

Betsey moved as elegantly as she knew how up the front porch, past her grandmother, past the cut glass in the front door, and up the same stairs she'd glided down to meet Eugene Boyd. In her room she laid her dress out as if it were covered with emeralds and pearls, diamonds and things. She might actually have a beau. Maybe Grandma was right, and Eugene Boyd had set his sights on little Miss Betsey Brown.

Jane rolled over in her bed. She'd spent most of the day putting her house back in order, missed work, missed her husband, missed her dreams of quiet and luxury, missed her version of mothering. Why do they have to be so much trouble? Why can't they just act right? Why aren't they lined up at the door in the morning all clean and silent. Oh silence. What she would give for an hour's silence. Greer would never understand. He *liked* noise. That's why he woke the house up with conga drums every morning. Tito Puente every evening for dinner music. Lee Morgan way into the night. No one in her house valued peace. Jane'd sent Charlie to the store for some Hershey's chocolates, where was he? Why did that boy always take twice as long to do a thing as anybody else would. There was nobody else she could depend on, besides Betsey.

"Elizabeth, come see your mother," Jane called down the hall. Betsey was lying next to her dress, imagining herself cheering for Eugene at the basketball game and then going to Mr. Robinson's where everybody could see them.

"What, Mama?" she whispered.

"Elizabeth, are you up here? Come into my room. I want to talk to you."

Of all the times to want to talk this was not one of them. Betsey'd been kissed. She didn't want to talk, she wanted to hold her mouth still just like when Eugene had kissed her. It was amazing that Grandma could have figured out what had been going on. Amazing how anyone sides Betsey and Eugene existed at all. Betsey wondered if Jane had felt her kissing and that's why she wanted to talk. Jane might have sensed it through the walls or the open windows, where the scents of dusk lingered and the laughter of the little children wrapped the screens in tinkling, bubbling surprises. Betsey ran her finger along the rim of her mouth to make sure it was there, right there that Eugene had kissed her. Kiss. She wanted to know more about kissing.

"Elizabeth, do you hear me? Come to my room right now. I want to tell you something."

Jane had no idea Betsey had done anything besides study her lessons and play rope or read like she usually did. Jane noticed a soft blush in her daughter's cheeks, but beyond that she saw a little girl with magic eyes and an impish smile that was hiding some huge secret.

"Elizabeth, what are you smiling about?"

"Oh, I'm just happy, Mama, that's all. I had a wonderful day. An absolutely wonderful day."

"Well, what happened?"

"Oh, nothing. Charlie and a friend of his came over

to play ball. I talked to Grandma. And it was just wonderful. That's all."

Jane motioned for Betsey to sit by her on the bed.

"Betsey, sweetheart, we're going to have to try really hard to keep the house straight and the children off your grandma's nerves until I can find someone to help out around here. I'm going to put an ad in the *St. Louis Argus* asking for someone who's good with children and can do light housework. I won't be accepting anybody off the streets again."

Betsey sank into her mother's arms. It hadn't been sucha wonderful day after all. There was good in it, like a kiss, and bad in it, like where was Miss Calhoun?

J U N E

J O R D A N

Ought to Be a Woman

Washing the floors to send you to college.
Staying at home so you can feel safe.
What do you think is the soul of her knowledge?
What is the aching of angels?

Biting her lips and lowering her eyes
to make sure there's food on the table.
What do you think would be her surprise
if the world were as willing as she's able.

Hugging herself in an old kitchen chair
  she listens
to your hurt and your rage.
What do you think she knows of despair?
What is the aching of age?

The father, the sister, the brother turn to her
and everybody white
turns to her.

What about her turning around alone in the everyday
light?

Ought to be a woman who can sit down, break down,
sit down
like everybody else call it quits on Sunday
Blues on Tuesday
Sleep until Monday—break down, sit down . . .

A way out of no way, it's flesh out of flesh
it's bravery kept locked inside.

A way out of no way it's too much to ask
too much of a task
for any one woman.

LANGSTON

HUGHES

Passing

Chicago,
Sunday, Oct. 10.

DEAR MA,

I felt like a dog, passing you downtown last night and not speaking to you. You were great, though. Didn't give a sign that you even knew me, let alone I was your son. If I hadn't had the girl with me, Ma, we might have talked. I'm not as scared as I used to be about somebody taking me for colored any more just because I'm seen talking on the street to a Negro. I guess in looks I'm sort of suspect-proof, anyway. You remember what a hard time I used to have in school trying to convince teachers I was really colored. Sometimes, even after they met you, my mother, they wouldn't believe it. They just thought I had a mulatto mammy, I guess. Since I've begun to pass for white, nobody has ever doubted that I am a white man. Where I work, the boss is a Southerner, and is always cussing out Negroes in my presence, not dreaming I'm one. It is to laugh!

Funny thing, though, Ma, how some white people certainly don't like colored people, do they? (If they did, then I wouldn't have to be passing to keep my good job.) They go out of their way sometimes to say bad things about colored folks, putting it out that all of us are thieves and liars, or else diseased—consumption and syphilis, and the like. No wonder it's hard for a black man to get a good job with that kind of false propaganda going around. I never knew they made a practice of saying such terrible things about us until I started passing and heard their conversations and lived their life.

But I don't mind being "white," Ma, and it was mighty generous of you to urge me to go ahead and make use of my light skin and good hair. It got me this job, Ma, where I still get $65 a week in spite of the depression. And I'm in line for promotion to the chief office secretary, if Mr. Weeks goes to Washington. When I look at the colored boy porter who sweeps out the office, I think that that's what I might be doing if I wasn't light-skinned enough to get by. No matter how smart that boy'd get to be, they wouldn't hire him for a clerk in the office, not if they knew it. Only for a porter. That's why I sometimes get a kick out of putting something over on the boss, who never dreams he's got a colored secretary.

But, Ma, I felt mighty bad about last night. The first time we'd met in public that way. That's the kind of thing that makes passing hard, having to deny your own family when you see them. Of course, I know you and I both realize it is all for the best, but anyhow it's terrible. I love you, Ma, and hate to do it, even if you say you don't mind.

But what did you think of the girl with me, Ma? She's the kid I'm going to marry. Pretty good looking, isn't she? Nice disposition. The parents are well fixed. Her folks are German Americans and don't have much prejudice about them, either. I took her to see a colored revue last week and she thought it was great. She said, "Darkies are so graceful and gay." I wonder what she would have said if I'd told her *I* was colored, or half-colored—that my old man was white, but you weren't? But I guess I won't go into that. Since I've made up my mind to live in the white world, and have found my place in it (a good place), why think about race any more? I'm glad I don't have to, I know that much.

I hope Charlie and Gladys don't feel bad about me. It's funny I was the only one of the kids light enough to pass. Charlie's darker than you, even, Ma. I know he sort of resented it in school when the teachers used to take me for white, before they knew we were brothers. I used to feel bad about it, too, then. But now I'm glad you backed me up, and told me to go ahead and get all I could out of life. That's what I'm going to do, Ma. I'm going to marry white and live white, and if any of my kids are born dark I'll swear they aren't mine. I won't get caught in the mire of color again. Not me. I'm free, Ma, free!

I'd be glad, though, if I could get away from Chicago,

transferred to the New York office, or the San Francisco branch of the firm—somewhere where what happened last night couldn't ever occur again. It was awful passing *you* and not speaking. And if Gladys or Charlie were to meet me in the street, they might not be as tactful as you were—because they don't seem to be very happy about my passing for white. I don't see why, though. I'm not hurting them any, and I send you money every week and help out just as much as they do, if not more. Tell them not to queer me, Ma, if they should ever run into me and the girlfriend any place. Maybe it would have been better if you and they had stayed in Cincinnati and I'd come away alone when we decided to move after the old man died. Or at least, we should have gone to different towns, shouldn't we?

Gee, Ma, when I think of how Papa left everything to his white family, and you couldn't legally do anything for us kids, my blood boils. You wouldn't have a chance in a Kentucky court, I know, but maybe if you'd tried anyway, his white children would have paid you something to shut up. Maybe they wouldn't want it known in the papers that they had colored brothers. But you was too proud, wasn't you, Ma? I wouldn't have been so proud.

Well, he did buy you a house and send all us kids through school. I'm glad I finished college in Pittsburgh before he died. It was too bad about Charlie and Glad having to drop out, but I hope Charlie gets something better to do than working in a garage. And from what you told me in your last letter about Gladys, I don't blame you for being worried about her—wanting to go in the chorus of one of those South Side cabarets. Lord! But I know it's really tough for girls to get any kind of job during this depression, especially for colored girls, even if Gladys is high yellow, and smart. But I hope you can keep her home, and out of those South Side dumps. They're no place for a good girl.

Well, Ma, I will close because I promised to take my weakness to the movies this evening. Isn't she sweet to look at, all blonde and blue-eyed? We're making plans about our house when we get married. We're going to take a little apartment on the North Side, in a good neighborhood, out on one of those nice quiet side streets where there are trees. I will take a box at the post office for your mail. Anyhow, I'm glad there's nothing to stop letters from crossing the color-line. Even if we can't meet often, we can write, can't we, Ma?

With love from your son,

JACK.

ANNA

DEAVERE

SMITH

Look in the Mirror

(Morning. Spring. A teen-age Black girl of Haitian descent. She has hair which is straightened, and is wearing a navy blue jumper and a white shirt. She is seated in a stairwell at her junior high school in Brooklyn.)

When I look in the mirror . . .
I don't know.
How did I find out I was Black . . .
(Tongue sound)
When I grew up and I look in the mirror and saw I was Black.
When I look at my parents,
That's how I knew I was Black.
Look at my skin.
You Black?
Black is beautiful.
I don't know.
That's what I always say.

I think White is beautiful too.
But I think Black is beautiful too.
In my class nobody is White, everybody's Black,
and some of them is Hispanic.
In my class
you can't call any of them Puerto Ricans.
They despise Puerto Ricans, I don't know why.
They think that Puerto Ricans are stuck up and
   everything.
They say, Oh my Gosh my nail broke, look at that cute
   guy and everything.
But they act like that themselves.
They act just like White girls.
Black girls is not like that.
Please, you should be in my class.
Like they say that Puerto Ricans act like that
and they don't see that they act like that themselves.
Black girls, they do bite off the Spanish girls,
they bite off of your clothes.
You don't know what that means? biting off?
Like biting off somebody's clothes
Like cop, following,
and last year they used to have a lot of girls like that.
They come to school with a style, right?
And if they see another girl with that style?
Oh my gosh look at her.
What she think she is,
she tryin' to bite off of me in some way
no don't be bitin' off of my sneakers

or like that.
Or doin' a hairstyle
I mean Black people are into hairstyles.
So they come to school, see somebody with a certain style,
they say uh-huh I'm gonna get me one just like that uh-huh,
that's the way Black people are
Yea-ah!
They don't like people doing that to them
and they do that to other people,
so the Black girls will follow the Spanish girls.
The Spanish girls don't bite off of us.
Some of the Black girls follow them.
But they don't mind
They don't care.
They follow each other.
Like there's three girls in my class,
they from the Dominican Republic.
They all stick together like glue.
They all three best friends.
They don't follow nobody,
like there's none of them lead or anything.
They don't hang around us either.
They're
by themselves.

I battered the cordons around me

And cradled my wings on the breeze

Then soared to the uttermost reaches

With rapture, with power, with ease!

—GEORGIA DOUGLAS JOHNSON

TONI

MORRISON

FROM

Sula

1922

IT WAS TOO COOL for ice cream. A hill wind was blowing dust and empty Camels wrappers about their ankles. It pushed their dresses into the creases of their behinds, then lifted the hems to peek at their cotton underwear. They were on their way to Edna Finch's Mellow House, an ice-cream parlor catering to nice folks—where even children would feel comfortable, you know, even though it was right next to Reba's Grill and just one block down from the Time and a Half Pool Hall. It sat in the curve of Carpenter's Road, which, in four blocks, made up all the sporting life available in the Bottom. Old men and young ones draped themselves in front of the Elmira Theater, Irene's Palace of Cosmetology, the pool hall, the grill, and the other sagging business enterprises that lined the street. On sills, on stoops, on crates, and broken chairs they sat tasting their teeth and waiting for something to distract them. Every passerby, every motorcar, every alteration in stance caught their attention and was commented on. Particularly they watched women. When a woman approached, the older men tipped their hats; the younger ones opened and closed their thighs. But all of them, whatever their age, watched her retreating view with interest.

Nel and Sula walked through this valley of eyes chilled by the wind and heated by the embarrassment of appraising stares. The old men looked at their stalk-like legs, dwelled on the cords in the backs of their knees, and remembered old dance steps they had not done in twenty years. In their lust, which age had turned to kindness, they moved their lips as though to stir up the taste of young sweat on tight skin.

Pig meat. The words were in all their minds. And one of them, one of the young ones, said it aloud. Softly but definitively and there was no mistaking the compliment. His name was Ajax, a twenty-one-year-old pool haunt of sinister beauty. Graceful and economical in every movement, he held a place of envy with men of all ages for his magnificently foul mouth. In fact he seldom cursed, and the epithets he chose were dull, even harmless. His reputation was derived from the way he handled the words. When he said "hell" he hit the *h* with his lungs and the impact was greater than the achievement of the most imaginative foul mouth in the town. He could say "shit" with a nastiness impossible to imitate. So, when he said "pig meat" as Nel and

Sula passed, they guarded their eyes lest someone see their delight.

It was not really Edna Finch's ice cream that made them brave the stretch of those panther eyes. Years later their own eyes would glaze as they cupped their chins in remembrance of the inchworm smiles, the squatting haunches, the track-rail legs straddling broken chairs. The cream-colored trousers marking with a mere seam the place where the mystery curled. Those smooth vanilla crotches invited them; those lemon-yellow gabardines beckoning to them.

They moved toward the ice-cream parlor like tightrope walkers, as thrilled by the possibility of a slip as by the maintenance of tension and balance. The least sideways glance, the merest toe stub, could pitch them into those creamy haunches spread wide with welcome. Somewhere beneath all of that daintiness, chambered in all that neatness, lay the thing that clotted their dreams.

Which was only fitting for it was in dreams that the two girls had first met. Long before Edna Finch's Mellow House opened, even before they marched through the chocolate halls of Garfield Primary School out onto the playground and stood facing each other through the ropes of the one vacant swing ("Go on." "No. You go."), they had already made each other's acquaintance in the delirium of their noon dreams. They were solitary little girls whose loneliness was so profound it intoxicated them and sent them stumbling into Technicolored visions that always included a presence, a someone, who, quite like the dreamer, shared the delight of the dream. When Nel, an only child, sat on the steps of her back porch surrounded by the high silence of her mother's incredibly orderly house, feeling the neatness pointing at her back, she studied the poplars and fell easily into a picture of herself lying on a flowered bed, tangled in her own hair, waiting for some fiery prince. He approached but never quite arrived. But always, watching the dream along with her, were some smiling sympathetic eyes. Someone as interested as she herself in the flow of her imagined hair, the thickness of the mattress of flowers, the voile sleeves that closed below her elbows in gold-threaded cuffs.

Similarly, Sula, also an only child, but wedged into a household of throbbing disorder constantly awry with things, people, voices, and the slamming of doors, spent hours in the attic behind a roll of linoleum galloping through her own mind on a gray-and-white horse tasting sugar and smelling roses in full view of a someone who shared both the taste and the speed.

So when they met, first in those chocolate halls and next through the ropes of the swing, they felt the ease and comfort of old friends. Because each had discovered years before that they were neither white nor male, and that all freedom and triumph was forbidden to them, they had set about creating something else to be. Their meeting was fortunate, for it let them use each other to grow on. Daughters of distant mothers and incomprehensible fathers (Sula's because he was dead; Nel's because he wasn't), they found in each other's eyes the intimacy they were looking for.

Nel Wright and Sula Peace were both twelve in 1922, wishbone thin and easy-assed. Nel was the color of wet sandpaper—just dark enough to escape the blows of the pitch-black truebloods and the contempt of old women who worried about such things as bad blood mixtures and knew that the origins of a mule and a mulatto were one and the same. Had she been any lighter-skinned she would have needed either her mother's protection on the way to school or a streak of mean to defend herself. Sula was a heavy brown with large quiet eyes, one of which featured a birthmark that spread from the middle of the lid toward the eyebrow, shaped something like a stemmed rose. It gave her otherwise plain face a broken excitement and blue-blade threat like the keloid scar of the razored man who sometimes played checkers with her grandmother. The birthmark was to grow darker as the years passed, but now it was the same shade as her gold-flecked eyes, which, to the end, were as steady and clean as rain.

Their friendship was as intense as it was sudden. They found relief in each other's personality. Although both were unshaped, formless things, Nel seemed stronger and more consistent than Sula, who could hardly be counted on to sustain any emotion for more than three minutes. Yet there was one time when that was not true, when she held on to a mood for weeks, but even that was in defense of Nel.

Four white boys in their early teens, sons of some newly arrived Irish people, occasionally entertained themselves in the afternoon by harassing black schoolchildren. With shoes that pinched and woolen knickers that made red rings on their calves, they had come to this valley with their parents believing as they did that it was a promised land—green and shimmering with welcome. What they found was a strange accent, a pervasive fear of their religion and firm resistance to their attempts to find work. With one exception the older residents of Medallion scorned them. The one exception was the black community. Although some of the Negroes had been in Medallion before the Civil War (the town didn't even have a name then), if they had any hatred for these newcomers it didn't matter because it didn't show. As a matter of fact, baiting them was the one activity that the white Protestant residents concurred in. In part their place in this world was secured only when they echoed the old residents' attitude toward blacks.

These particular boys caught Nel once, and pushed her from hand to hand until they grew tired of the frightened helpless face. Because of that incident, Nel's route home from school became elaborate. She, and then Sula, managed to duck them for weeks until a chilly day in November when Sula said, "Let's us go on home the shortest way."

Nel blinked, but acquiesced. They walked up the street until they got to the bend of Carpenter's Road where the boys lounged on a disused well. Spotting their prey, the boys sauntered forward as though there were nothing in the world on their minds but the gray sky. Hardly able to control their grins, they stood like a gate blocking the path. When the girls were three feet in front of the boys, Sula reached into her coat pocket and pulled out Eva's paring knife. The boys stopped short, exchanged looks and dropped all pretense of innocence. This was going to be better than they thought. They were going to try and fight back, and with a knife. Maybe they could get an arm around one of their waists, or tear . . .

Sula squatted down in the dirt road and put everything down on the ground: her lunchpail, her reader, her mittens, her slate. Holding the knife in her right hand, she pulled the slate toward her and pressed her left forefinger down hard on its edge. Her aim was determined but inaccurate. She slashed off only the tip of her finger. The four boys stared open-mouthed at the wound and the scrap of flesh, like a button mushroom, curling in the cherry blood that ran into the corners of the slate.

Sula raised her eyes to them. Her voice was quiet. "If I can do that to myself, what you suppose I'll do to you?"

The shifting dirt was the only way Nel knew that they were moving away; she was looking at Sula's face, which seemed miles and miles away.

But toughness was not their quality—adventuresomeness was—and a mean determination to explore everything that interested them, from one-eyed chickens high-stepping in their penned yards to Mr. Buckland Reed's gold teeth, from the sound of sheets flapping in the wind to the labels on Tar Baby's wine bottles. And they had no priorities. They could be distracted from watching a fight with mean razors by the glorious smell of hot tar being poured by roadmen two hundred yards away.

In the safe harbor of each other's company they could afford to abandon the ways of other people and concentrate on their own perceptions of things. When Mrs. Wright reminded Nel to pull her nose, she would do it enthusiastically but without the least hope in the world.

"While you sittin' there, honey, go 'head and pull your nose."

"It hurts, Mamma."

"Don't you want a nice nose when you grow up?"

After she met Sula, Nel slid the clothespin under the blanket as soon as she got in the bed. And although there was still the hateful hot comb to suffer through each Saturday evening, its consequences—smooth hair—no longer interested her.

Joined in mutual admiration they watched each day

as though it were a movie arranged for their amusement. The new theme they were now discovering was men. So they met regularly, without even planning it, to walk down the road to Edna Finch's Mellow House, even though it was too cool for ice cream.

RANDALL

KENAN

FROM

A Visitation of Spirits

December 8, 1985
8:45 a.m.

"LORD, LORD, LORD," she said.

The first time she slipped on the grass and fell that morning, he rushed to her, but she shooed him away and clambered, slowly, to her feet. But then, after a few precious steps, she fell again.

"Lord, Lord, Lord."

This time she just sat there on the frost-covered lawn, between her house and Jimmy's car, her head hung down, her eyes closed.

"You okay, Aunt Ruth? You want some help?"

Jimmy stood less than two feet from his great-aunt, but he hesitated. When he walked up to her and stooped over to pick her up, she opened her eyes and shot him a look that sent slivers of ice through his veins.

"I'm fine! Leave me be! I can get up on my own. Just leave me a spell."

Reluctantly, Jimmy stepped back and watched her jam her cane into the earth as though she were driving a stake, and, after getting up onto her knees, put one foot on the ground and stop.

"Help her, boy."

From the car Zeke called to Jimmy. He leaned out the window from the front seat of the blue Oldsmobile and watched the old woman with impatience. Like her, he was wearing Sunday-go-to-meeting best; his fedora, perhaps as old as he, sat in his lap.

"I don't need no help, Ezekiel Cross!"

"You do, Ruth. Let this boy help you."

"I been standing up on my own for ninety-two years and I—"

"Yeah, but look like you ain't doing too good a job right now."

Her cane slipped again and down she went with an umph and a sigh like grey.

This time she offered no resistance when Jimmy gently lifted her to her feet and dusted off her clothes. She stood still at first, her brow covered with sweat, though the air was frigid. Taking her first step like a calf trying out new legs, slowly, more and more confidently, she walked to the car.

"Just old," she finally mumbled to herself. "Just old."

"You need any help getting in, Aunt Ruth?"

Ignoring Jimmy, she slid her cane onto the floor of the backseat first, and holding onto the door frame as though a mighty wind might come along and snatch her away, she eased into the car, head first. Sitting, she pulled her legs in with great effort. Once in, puffing and wheezing and wiping away the sweat on her forehead, she impatiently motioned for Jimmy to close the door.

Without saying a word, Jimmy got into the car, closed the door, and started down the dirt road.

"Cold today, ain't it?" Zeke yawned.

"Yes, but the weatherman says it should warm up some. Said it's going to rain too."

Ruth grunted. She stared out over the empty fields as the car drove past, her hands folded like heavy rags in her lap.

A flock of black birds with red-tipped wings covered a field to the left. When the car passed they rose, as one, squawking and chirping, into the air, a sheer black cloth caught up in the wind, the tips of their wings crimson flashes. The black cloud sailed up and over the road, over the car, into the wood on the other side, fitting onto the tree limbs like black Christmas ornaments.

"Ain't gone rain. It's gone snow."

"You think it will, Aunt Ruth?"

"Ruth," Zeke glanced back at her and clicked his mouth. "You know it ain't gone snow in no December."

Ruth made her own clicking sound. " 'Think.' Think? Boy, in all my ninety-some years, I spect I can tell when it's gone snow or no. You see a sky like it is, and then on top of that see a swarm of them red-tipped blackbirds on the ground like that— You just wait and see. Besides. I feels it in my bones." She turned and looked out the window.

"Lord, Ruth, you make it sound like you know everything once you pass ninety."

"Well, you just get to ninety and see for yourself."

"I ain't got but six years."

In a short while they passed a few cars lined up on the road, near the entrance to a driveway. Yet, more cars were in the driveway and in the yard of the white, A-framed house. People were milling all about the yard.

Smoke rose off from the side of the house. Men congregated out near the barn; women stood around under the shed a few yards from the house.

Zeke perked up. "Hog killing. Did you all know Bud Stokes was going to have a hog killing today?"

"No."

"Of course," Ruth said, scoldingly. "How can you live right here and not know somebody was having a hog killing? Nosey as you is?"

"You all want to stop?" Jimmy looked at his watch.

"No." Ruth looked the other way. "Seen enough hog killings to last me another ninety-two years. Sides. I wants to get this here trip over and done with. Don't like no long trip in no car, no how."

"You, Uncle Zeke?"

Zeke looked out at the busy yard with the yearning of a sailor for the sea. "You heard her, boy. Drive on."

Soon the car turned off the dirt road onto the highway and drove on.

Advent
(or The Beginning of the End)

You've been to a hog killing before, haven't you? They don't happen as often as they once did. People simply don't raise hogs like they used to.

Once, in this very North Carolina town, practically everyone with a piece of land kept a hog or two, at least. And come the cold months of December and January folk would begin to butcher and salt and smoke and pickle. In those days a hog was a mighty good thing to have, to see you through the winter. But you know all this, don't you?

Remember how excited all the children would be on hog-killing day? Running about, gnawing at cracklings. A tan-and-black mongrel would be snarling and barking and tugging with a German shepherd over some bloody piece of meat. People would be rushing about, here and yon. The men would crowd about the hogpen, the women would stand around long tables under a shed, and somewhere in the yard huge iron cauldrons full of water would boil and boil, stoked with oak and pine timber. The air would be thick with smoke and the smell of sage and pepper and cooked meats and blood. You can even smell it now, I'm sure.

Do you recall the two or three women who stand out in the middle of the field—a field not planted in the winter rye grass that has just begun to peek from the stiff earth? They stand about the hole the men dug the day before, a hole as deep and as wide as a grave. The women stand there at its edge: one holds a huge intestine that looks more like a monstrous, hairless caterpillar. She squeezes the thing from top to bottom, time after time, forcing all the foul matter down and out, into the hole; and when the bulk is through the second woman pours steaming hot water dipped from a bucket into one end of the fleshy sac as the other woman holds it steady. She sloshes the gut gently back and forth, back and forth like a balloon full of water, until she finally slings the nasty gray water into the reeking hole in the ground. All the while they talk, their faces placid, their fingers deft, their aprons splattered with fecal matter, the hole sending steam up into the air like a huge cooking pot, reeking, stinking.

Surely someone told you of the huge vat of water over the fire, the blue-red flames licking the sides. Here they will dunk the fat corpses, to scald the skin and hair. Four men, two on either end of two chains, will roll, heave-ho, the thing over into the vat and then round and round and round in the boiling water, until you can reach down and yank out hair by the handfuls. They will roll the creature out and scrape it clean of hair and skin, and it will be pinkish white like the bellies of dead fish. They will bind and skewer its hind feet with a thick wooden peg, drag it over by the old smokehouse, and then hoist it up onto a pole braced high, higher than a man.

Then someone will take a great silver knife and

make a thin true line down the belly of the beast, from the rectum to the top of its throat. He will make a deep incision at the top and with a wet and ripping sound like the bursting of a watermelon, the creature will be split clear in two, its delicate organs spilling down like vomit, the fine, shiny sacs waiting there to be cut loose, one by one. The blood left in the hog will drip from its snout, in slow, long drips, dripping, staining the brown winter grass a deep maroon. But I'm certain you've witnessed all this, of course . . .

At the same time, beneath the shed, the women would be busy, with knives, with grinders, with spoons and forks; the greasy tables littered with salts and peppers and spices, hunks of meat, bloody and in pans to be made into sausages, pans of cooked liver to be made into liver pudding. Remember the odor of cooking meats and spices, so thick, so heady? Remember the women talking? Their jabber is constant and unchecked, rising and falling, recollection and gossip, observation and complaint, in and out, out and in, round and round, the rhythm, the chant, a chaotic symphony.

I need not tell you of the hog pen? It will be a fenced-off place with a shelter jutting off from the barn. The hogs will all be closed off in their stalls. And the men will stand around the fence, talking, gossiping, bragging, complaining in the crisp air, their breath rising, converging in a cloud about their heads, and vanishing.

Some older man will give a young boy a gun, perhaps, and instruct him not to be afraid, to take his time, to aim straight. The men will all look at one another and the boy with a sense of mutual pride, as the man goes over to the gate and with some effort moves the three slats that close off the hogpen. Then with a beanpole he beats all the hogs back except for the largest, and he will proceed to corral it into the outside area, saying: Gee there, Hog! Whoa! Get, now, get! The hog, a rusty, rough-hided, brown hog, shambles out into the yard and trips over a plank, letting out an all-too-human, fat sigh as its belly hits the ground. The man pops it on the behind with the beanpole and it clambers quickly to its feet with a grunt, a snort, a squeal. It circles the fence, eyeing the standing men with something less than suspicion.

Then the hog will stop and uncannily eye the boy who holds the gun, unmoving and solid; you might say it resembles a rhinoceros or an elephant about to charge. It lets out another snort, steam jetting into the cold air. But it remains still. Its eyes are tiny and mean, but bewildered just the same. The boy will, carefully, take his aim slowly, slowly, taking his time. He squeezes. The gun fires. The hog jumps, snorts: you will see a red dot appear on the broad plain between the eyes, hear the bang of the gun. The hog rears up on its hind legs like a horse, bucking, tossing its head, but only once, twice. It seems to land miraculously on its front legs, but only for a split second. It topples, hitting the ground with a thud, and lets out a sound that you might call a death rattle—all in a matter of seconds. Its eyes fix intensely on nothing. Its breathing comes labored; the dot in its forehead runs red. The man pulls out a long, silver knife, rushes to the expiring mound, catches the flesh under the thing's great head, and, with a very steady hand, makes a deep and long incision in its throat, slicing the artery there. The thick, deep-red blood, steaming in the cold December air, gushes, bathing his hands and shoes. The hog shivers: trembles: quakes: its legs spasm and thrust in the air like a sleeping dog's until, in a few minutes, it ceases to twitch, lying in a pool of red.

But you've seen this, haven't you? When you were younger? Perhaps . . .

Of course it's a way of life that has evaporated. You'd be hard-pressed to find a hogpen these days, let alone a hog. No, folk nowadays go to the A&P for their sausages, to the Winn Dixie for their liver pudding, to the Food Lion for their cured ham. Nobody seems to eat pickled pig's feet anymore and chitlins are . . .

But the ghosts of those times are stubborn; and though the hog stalls are empty, a herd can be heard, trampling the grasses and flowers and fancy bushes, trampling the foreign trees of the new families, living in their new homes. A ghostly herd waiting to be butchered.

CLAUDE

MCKAY

If We Must Die

If we must die—let it not be like hogs
Hunted and penned in an inglorious spot,
While round us bark the mad and hungry dogs,
Making their mock at our accursed lot.
If we must die—oh, let us noble die,
So that our precious blood may not be shed
In vain; that even the monsters we defy
Shall be constrained to honor us though dead!
Oh, Kinsmen! We must meet the common foe;
Though far outnumbered, let us show us brave,
And for their thousand blows deal one deathblow!
What though before us lies the open grave?
Like men we'll face the murderous, cowardly pack,
Pressed to the wall, dying, but fighting back!

NIKKI

GIOVANNI

Legacies

her grandmother called her from the playground
        "yes, ma'am"
        "i want chu to learn how to make rolls" said the old
woman proudly
but the little girl didn't want
to learn how because she knew
even if she couldn't say it that
that would mean when the old one died she would
    be less
dependent on her spirit so
she said
        "i don't want to know how to make no rolls"
with her lips poked out
and the old woman wiped her hands on
her apron saying "lord
        these children"
and neither of them ever
said what they meant
and i guess nobody ever does.

GWENDOLYN

BROOKS

FROM

Maud Martha

home

WHAT HAD BEEN wanted was this always, this always to last, the talking softly on this porch, with the snake plant in the jardiniere in the southwest corner, and the obstinate slip from Aunt Eppie's magnificent Michigan fern at the left side of the friendly door. Mama, Maud Martha, and Helen rocked slowly in their rocking chairs, and looked at the late afternoon light on the lawn, and at the emphatic iron of the fence and at the poplar tree. These things might soon be theirs no longer. Those shafts and pools of light, the tree, the graceful iron, might soon be viewed possessively by different eyes.

Papa was to have gone that noon, during his lunch hour, to the office of the Home Owners' Loan. If he had not succeeded in getting another extension, they would be leaving this house in which they had lived for more than fourteen years. There was little hope.

The Home Owners' Loan was hard. They sat, making their plans.

"We'll be moving into a nice flat somewhere," said Mama. "Somewhere on South Park, or Michigan, or in Washington Park Court." Those flats, as the girls and Mama knew well, were burdens on wages twice the size of Papa's. This was not mentioned now.

"They're much prettier than this old house," said Helen. "I have friends I'd just as soon not bring here. And I have other friends that wouldn't come down this far for anything, unless they were in a taxi."

Yesterday, Maud Martha would have attacked her. Tomorrow she might. Today she said nothing. She merely gazed at a little hopping robin in the tree, her tree, and tried to keep the fronts of her eyes dry.

"Well, I do know," said Mama, turning her hands over and over, "that I've been getting tireder and tireder of doing that firing. From October to April, there's firing to be done."

"But lately we've been helping, Harry and I," said Maud Martha. "And sometimes in March and April and in October, and even in November, we could build a little fire in the fireplace. Sometimes the weather was just right for that."

She knew, from the way they looked at her, that this had been a mistake. They did not want to cry.

But she felt that the little line of white, somewhat ridged with smoked purple, and all that cream-shot saffron, would never drift across any western sky except that in back of this house. The rain would drum with as sweet a dullness nowhere but here. The birds on South Park were mechanical birds, no better than the poor caught canaries in those "rich" women's sun parlors.

"It's just going to kill Papa!" burst out Maud Martha. "He loves this house! He *lives* for this house!"

"He lives for us," said Helen. "It's us he loves. He wouldn't want the house, except for us."

"And he'll have us," added Mama, "wherever."

"You know," Helen sighed, "if you want to know the truth, this is a relief. If this hadn't come up, we would have gone on, just dragged on, hanging out here forever."

"It might," allowed Mama, "be an act of God. God may just have reached down, and picked up the reins."

"Yes," Maud Martha cracked in, "that's what you always say—that God knows best."

Her mother looked at her quickly, decided the statement was not suspect, looked away.

Helen saw Papa coming. "There's Papa," said Helen.

They could not tell a thing from the way Papa was walking. It was that same dear little staccato walk, one shoulder down, then the other, then repeat, and repeat. They watched his progress. He passed the Kennedys', he passed the vacant lot, he passed Mrs. Blakemore's. They wanted to hurl themselves over the fence, into the street, and shake the truth out of his collar. He opened his gate—the gate—and still his stride and face told them nothing.

"Hello," he said.

Mama got up and followed him through the front door. The girls knew better than to go in too.

Presently Mama's head emerged. Her eyes were lamps turned on.

"It's all right," she exclaimed. "He got it. It's all over. Everything is all right."

The door slammed shut. Mama's footsteps hurried away.

"I think," said Helen, rocking rapidly, "I think I'll give a party. I haven't given a party since I was eleven. I'd like some of my friends to just casually see that we're homeowners."

B E R N I C E
J O H N S O N
R E A G O N

I Remember, I Believe

I don't know how my mother walked her trouble down
I don't know how my father stood his ground
I don't know how my people survived slavery
I do remember, that's why I believe

I don't know why the rivers overflow their banks
I don't know why the snow falls and covers the ground
I don't know why the hurricane sweeps thru the land
every now and then
Standing in a rainstorm, I believe

I don't know why the angels woke me up this morning
soon
I don't know why the blood still runs through my veins
I don't know how I rate to run another day
I am here still running, I believe

My God calls to me in the morning dew
The power of the universe knows my name
Gave me a song to sing and sent me on my way
I raise my voice for justice, I believe

About the Contributors

After his close friend committed suicide by jumping from the George Washington Bridge into the Hudson River, JAMES BALDWIN moved to Paris in the 1940s with the hopes of leaving America's racist ideals behind him and pursuing his writing career. He would later become known as one of America's most celebrated authors. Among his most noted works of fiction are *If Beale Street Could Talk*, *Another Country*, and *Go Tell It on the Mountain*.

TONI CADE BAMBARA authored a short story collection, *The Seabirds Are Still Alive*, and the novel *The Salt Eaters*, which won a National Book Award. It was her book of stories, *Gorilla, My Love*, first published in 1971, that hooked me into her. I was in seventh-grade English class when a mimeographed copy of the title story appeared on my desk one morning. Having spent years going back and forth between New York and

South Carolina, I was familiar with the vivid images of uncles and grandparents and hot sweaty cars on long stretches of highway. And too, at the core of the story is a strong-willed girl with a broken heart: It speaks to the strengths and weaknesses in all of us. Toni Cade Bambara died in 1995. She leaves behind a legacy of beautifully written prose.

PAUL BEATTY's collection of poetry *Big Bank Take Little Bank* was voted a Best Book of 1991 by the *Village Voice.* In Brooklyn, he is best known as the poetry slammer. In 1990, Beatty was a New York Poetry Slam Winner. He's been on MTV and in numerous anthologies including *Norton Anthology NEXT: Young American Writings of the New Generation.* In 1996, Beatty's stunning first novel, *The White Boy Shuffle,* was published. "Big Bowls of Cereal" appears in his poetry collection *Joker, Joker, Deuce.*

GWENDOLYN BROOKS is "old school"—as my little sister would say—one of the greats who started us on the road to this place. *A Street in Bronzeville*, a collection of poetry, was published in 1945. Five years later, she won a Pulitzer Prize for *Annie Allen*—the first time the prize had been awarded to an African American for a poetry collection. *Maud Martha*, her first novel, has the same poetic force and beauty as her poetry.

The first time we watched the televised version of ERNEST J. GAINES's *The Autobiography of Miss Jane Pittman*, starring Cicely Tyson, my grandmother and I sat down in front of the television and cried. We didn't know if Miss Jane Pittman was real or not, but we knew someone like her had lived somewhere. Years later, I would find out that the author of this book that the television show was adapted from was a man, a Louisianian by the name of Gaines whose brilliant works included *A Gathering of Old Men, In My Father's House, A Long Day in November, Of Love and Dust, Catherine Carmier*, and *A Lesson Before Dying*. Gaines's work often confronts the racial tensions of the South with tenderness and compassion.

NIKKI GIOVANNI was one of the first poets I ever loved. I was ten the first time I got my hands on *Spin a Soft Black Song*. Of course I stole it from the library. Of course my mother found it. Of course I was made to use my allowance to pay the overdue fines. But that was a long time ago. Her poem "Ego Tripping" (from *Ego Tripping and Other Poems for Young Readers*) made me proud to be Black and female. Once I saw her on a show on channel thirteen and sat mesmerized while she read to me from the small black-and-white TV screen. When I started putting this anthology together, I called my grandmother and asked her to check the bookshelves for any books that I might be able to use. She sent Giovanni's *My House*, the dog-eared copy I owned as a child. In it, I found "Legacies" and remembered it from childhood—remembered my grandmother reading it to me.

ROSA GUY's novel *Ruby* provided me with one of my earliest introductions to beautiful, strong African American women. I fell in love with the character Daphne Duprey, who prided herself with being "cool, calm, collected, poised, sophisticated, cultured, and refined." Daphne had an afro and an amazing mind. I quickly became a Rosa Guy fan, tearing through her trilogy that included *The Friends, Edith Jackson*, and *Ruby*. Later I found out that Rosa Guy was one of the founders of the Harlem Writers' Guild and lived in New York.

LANGSTON HUGHES's *The Ways of White Folks* was one of my favorite books as a young person. Half of his inferences I didn't understand and the other half, my big sister took the time to explain to me. I loved the simplicity of his language. It reminded me of his poetry, which I knew well. His poetry has been widely anthologized, translated, and illustrated. *The Sweet Flypaper of Life* described in words and photographs (by Roy DeCarava) the extraordinary everyday lives of African Americans in Harlem. Hughes's "I, Too" was a poem I had to memorize for a third-grade assembly, although at the time I had no idea what I was saying or why. Years later, I would read the poem again and "get it."

Langston Hughes's other works include *Not Without Laughter* and *The Weary Blues.*

The poem used to separate the sections of this anthology is titled "Your World" and was written by GEORGIA DOUGLAS JOHNSON, who lived from 1886–1966. She studied music at Oberlin Conservatory with dreams of becoming a composer. Published collections of her lyrics include *The Heart of a Woman* (1918), *Bronze* (1922), and *Share My World* (1962).

JUNE JORDAN's "Ought to Be a Woman" was put to music by Sweet Honey in the Rock, an all-black, all-female a cappella group. A poet and an essayist, June Jordan is the author of the libretto "I Was Looking at the Ceiling and Then I Saw the Sky." Her collections of essays include *Civil Wars* and *Technical Difficulties.*

RANDALL KENAN's debut novel *A Visitation of Spirits* was the book it seemed everyone was talking about back in 1989. And with good reason—it's flawless. And more than this, it moves away from the traditional style of the conventional narrative. I am so grateful that Kenan is breaking ground for other new writers whose work transcends the traditional.

JAMAICA KINCAID is the author of a number of fine works, including *Lucy, Annie John, A Small Place*, and, most recently, *Autobiography of My Mother*. I received *Annie*

John as a birthday present one year and the story "Gwen," which is part of *Annie John*, has been one of my favorites ever since.

CLAUDE MCKAY's works include his autobiography, *A Long Way from Home*, and *Harlem Shadows: The Poems of Claude McKay*. He lived from 1890 to 1948. After *Harlem Shadows* (1922), Claude McKay published only prose, although he did continue to write poetry. I read "If We Must Die" for the first time as a teenager and was surprised that it was the complete opposite of what I had been raised to believe was the right thing to do—which was "turn the other cheek."

In 1993 TONI MORRISON received the Nobel Prize for Literature. Finally! The first African American woman to receive this high honor, Morrison is the author of six novels, *The Bluest Eye, Tar Baby, Beloved, Sula, Song of Solomon*, and *Jazz*. Like James Baldwin and Ernest Gaines, Morrison is on my "Brilliant" shelf.

DR. BERNICE JOHNSON REAGON founded the group Sweet Honey in the Rock. She was a strong force in the Civil Rights Movement and many of the group's songs reflect her beliefs of nonviolence, equality, and justice. Many songs, like "I Remember, I Believe," speak to the importance of keeping the memory of our past alive. A recipient of the prestigious MacArthur Fellowship, Dr.

Reagon is currently curator of the Museum of American History at the Smithsonian Institution.

TIM SEIBLES was born in Philadelphia in 1955. He moved to Dallas in 1973 then on to Vermont to receive his MFA in writing. I met him at the Fine Arts Work Center, where we were both writing fellows, living in Provincetown, confronting the long Cape Cod winter ahead of us. In the years that we lived in Provincetown, we became good friends, reading each other's work, talking poetry and fiction over midnight potluck dinners. Now Tim's an associate professor at Old Dominion in Virginia and I'm living in New York. Recently, I received his latest book of poetry, *Kerosene*, in the mail. I read it through in one sitting and now it sits beside his other books of poetry, *Body Moves* and *Hurdy Gurdy*. He is brilliant. I'm glad he is a friend of mine.

NTOZAKE SHANGE'S *for colored girls who have considered suicide/when the rainbow is enuf* peeled itself back to reveal a distinguished playwright at its core. "Nappy Edges" and "A Daughter's Geography" showed us we had a poet in our midst. *Sassafras, Cypress & Indigo,* and *Betsey Brown* introduced Ntozake as a novelist. She does it all. Brilliantly.

ANNA DEAVERE SMITH'S *Fire in the Mirrors* was first performed at The Public Theater in New York under the direction of George C. Wolfe. Smith interviewed a number of people who had in some way been involved in a clash between Blacks and Jews in the Crown Heights section of Brooklyn in August 1991. The piece spoke to the rage and misunderstanding on both sides. Later, Smith would perform *Twilight*, again using interviews of real people to translate the story of the Los Angeles riots of 1992.

JACQUELINE WOODSON is the author of nine critically acclaimed books for adults and young adults: *Martin Luther King, Jr., Last Summer with Maizon, The Dear One, Maizon at Blue Hill, Between Madison and Palmetto, Book Chase, I Hadn't Meant to Tell You This, Autobiography of a Family Photo,* and *From the Notebooks of Melanin Sun.* She has won numerous awards for her writing, including two Coretta Scott King Honors, a Jane Addams Children's Book Award, *Booklist*'s Editor's Choice Award, *Kenyon Review*'s Award for Literary Excellence in Fiction, and two Lambda Literary Awards. She has held teaching positions at Goddard College and Eugene Lang College, and frequently travels around the country to talk about her work.

Jacqueline Woodson makes her home in Brooklyn, New York.